See You in Seattle

By:
Brooke St. James

See You in Seattle

Published in Nashville, Tennessee, by Elm Hill, an imprint of Thomas Nelson. Elm Hill and Thomas Nelson are registered trademarks of HarperCollins Christian Publishing, Inc.

Elm Hill titles may be purchased in bulk for educational, business, fund-raising, or sales promotional use. For information, please e-mail SpecialMarkets@ThomasNelson.com.

ISBN 978-1-4003-3938-9

Table of Contents

Other titles available from Brooke St. James:

Another Shot:
(A Modern-Day Ruth and Boaz Story)

When Lightning Strikes

Something of a Storm (All in Good Time #1)
Someone Someday (All in Good Time #2)

Finally My Forever (Meant for Me #1)
Finally My Heart's Desire (Meant for Me #2)
Finally My Happy Ending (Meant for Me #3)

Shot by Cupid's Arrow

Dreams of Us

Meet Me in Myrtle Beach (Hunt Family #1)
Kiss Me in Carolina (Hunt Family #2)
California's Calling (Hunt Family #3)
Back to the Beach (Hunt Family #4)
It's About Time (Hunt Family #5)

Loved Bayou (Martin Family #1)
Dear California (Martin Family #2)
My One Regret (Martin Family #3)
Broken and Beautiful (Martin Family #4)
Back to the Bayou (Martin Family #5)

Almost Christmas

JFK to Dublin (Shower & Shelter Artist Collective #1)
Not Your Average Joe (Shower & Shelter Artist Collective #2)
So Much for Boundaries (Shower & Shelter Artist Collective #3)
Suddenly Starstruck (Shower & Shelter Artist Collective #4)
Love Stung (Shower & Shelter Artist Collective #5)
My American Angel (Shower & Shelter Artist Collective #6)

Summer of '65 (Bishop Family #1)
Jesse's Girl (Bishop Family #2)
Maybe Memphis (Bishop Family #3)
So Happy Together (Bishop Family #4)
My Little Gypsy (Bishop Family #5)
Malibu by Moonlight (Bishop Family #6)
The Harder They Fall (Bishop Family #7)
Come Friday (Bishop Family #8)
Something Lovely (Bishop Family #9)

So This is Love (Miami Stories #1)
All In (Miami Stories #2)
Something Precious (Miami Stories #3)

The Suite Life (The Family Stone #1)
Feels Like Forever (The Family Stone #2)
Treat You Better (The Family Stone #3)
The Sweetheart of Summer Street (The Family Stone #4)
Out of Nowhere (The Family Stone #5)

Delicate Balance (Blair Brothers #1)
Cherished (Blair Brothers #2)
The Whole Story (Blair Brothers #3)
Dream Chaser (Blair Brothers #4)

Kiss & Tell (Novella) (Tanner Family #0)
Mischief & Mayhem (Tanner Family #1
Reckless & Wild (Tanner Family #2)
Heart & Soul (Tanner Family #3)
Me & Mister Everything (Tanner Family #4)
Through & Through (Tanner Family #5)
Lost & Found (Tanner Family #6)
Sparks & Embers (Tanner Family #7)
Young & Wild (Tanner Family #8)

Easy Does It (Bank Street Stories #1)
The Trouble with Crushes (Bank Street Stories #2)
A King for Christmas (Novella) (A Bank Street Christmas)
Diamonds Are Forever (Bank Street Stories #3)
Secret Rooms and Stolen Kisses (Bank Street Stories #4)
Feels Like Home (Bank Street Stories #5)
Just Like Romeo and Juliet (Bank Street Stories #6)
See You in Seattle (Bank Street Stories #7)
The Sweetest Thing (Bank Street Stories #8)
Back to Bank Street (Bank Street Stories #9)

Split Decision (How to Tame a Heartbreaker #1)
B-Side (How to Tame a Heartbreaker #2)

Cole for Christmas

Somewhere in Seattle (Alexander Family #1)
Wildest Dream (Alexander Family #2)
About to Fall (Alexander Family #3)

Hope for the Best (Morgan Family #1)
Full Circle (Morgan Family #2)
Just for Tonight (Morgan Family #3)
Way Past Mistletoe (Morgan Family #4)
The Wild One (Morgan Family #5)
The Rest is History (Morgan Family #6)
Two Is Better Than One (Morgan Family #7)

Chapter 1

Summer
Seattle, Washington

Mac Klein, son of Lucy and Drew Klein, firstborn grandchild of Daniel and Abby King.

Mac was the passionate one.

He didn't necessarily see that as his number one attribute, but he knew it was an apt description because he had heard people say that about him his whole life. He was constantly surrounded by family and friends, and he had heard them all describe him as being passionate.

Mac was just himself, so being passionate must've come naturally to him. He certainly had focus and determination. He lived a lifestyle of hard work, and he could now call himself a veteran NFL player. Mac had six successful seasons under his belt and was going into his seventh. He had been with the Seattle Seahawks for his entire career, and he had made a home in the city and a place for himself in the role of backup quarterback. He was a team player and a natural encourager, and his attitude and work ethic played a crucial role in the Seahawks' locker room morale. Mac had a good contract and a good relationship with his team—players, staff, and coaches. He was playing professional football at the highest level, and he loved it. The team didn't depend on him to make all the key plays every game, but Mac's role was extremely important, and he knew it. He had to be ready all the time.

He had to come in clutch when the team needed him, and he was good at that. He thrived in high-pressure situations. And when he wasn't in the game, he kept the first-string quarterback encouraged and pumped up. The attitude part of it came easier to Mac, but he wasn't a bad football player, either.

It wasn't a secret that Drew wasn't Mac's biological dad. Mac didn't grow up knowing his real dad, but he had met him a couple of times since high school and he knew that the guy, Bradley, was an athlete—a college football player.

Bradley had called some since Mac made it to the NFL, but Mac got the feeling that he wanted something from him every time they talked. He wasn't obnoxious about it, but Mac also kept a little distance, based on the vibe he got from him.

His actual dad, Drew, the man who adopted and raised him, was a judge in Galveston, Texas. The majority of his family still lived in this small, island town. Most of Mac's memories from growing up were of Houston, but his early childhood was spent in Galveston, and his parents were living there again, near other members of his huge family.

His grandparents and aunts and uncles had property in Galveston, and there were always dozens of people at his family gatherings. Mac had to miss the holidays every year, but he got time off in the spring and early summer, and he was able to go home to Texas and catch up with his family.

He also got to see his family when they came to visit. He had lived in Seattle long enough that different members of the family made a routine of coming up to see him at various times of the year. He practically had someone visiting at every game.

It was because of this that Mac bought a large, six-bedroom home. It was that, and the fact that the house was on Bank Street, which seemed like a sign to Mac at the time. His family owned businesses up and down Bank Street in Galveston, and when the house came on the market, Mac bought it in spite of it being too large for a single guy.

It didn't, however, stay too large for long. It was like women, no matter what size purse they have, they fill it up. The same went with Mac's house. It was too big when he bought it, and then people moved in.

It started a couple of years ago when two of his cousins, Ozzy and Bri, came to live with him because they wanted to go to college in Seattle. He was a decade older than most of his cousins, and they all looked up to him, but Ozzy was the first one to have the idea of going to college where Mac lived. Their other cousin, Bri, jumped on the idea when word got to her. Ozzy and Bri moved in two years ago, and now they were going into their junior year at the University of Washington.

Then, earlier this year, Mac's little sister, Katie, took a job in Seattle and moved in with Mac as well.

And the partridge in a pear tree of this story, the last person to move into Mac's house, was Justin Teague. As of two weeks ago, the new, young teammate, was also a roommate.

Ozzy and Bri were currently away. They had gone back to Galveston for a few weeks since it was summer. But both of them worked jobs in Seattle, and they would be back next week.

Mac currently had two people, Katie and Justin, living in his home. But when Ozzy and Bri got back there would be four. It would be the most he had ever had living with him at once, but he didn't mind at all. That meant he only had one extra bedroom for out-of-town visitors, but he figured people could sleep on couches if it came to it. Mac was in the process of building an apartment over his detached garage, but for now, everyone would be in the main house.

He liked having a full house. They were all people he knew and loved. Justin was the only one Mac wasn't close to for very long, but sometimes you just know you get along with certain people, and that was how it was with Justin. Mac had that type of connection with a few other teammates over the years.

Everyone living in the house was respectful and pitched in, and Mac was happy to be the person with a place big enough to accommodate family and friends.

They didn't bother him, anyway. He had a giant master suite, with a private lap pool, and all he had to do was disappear into it if he wanted some time alone.

You might be wondering how a backup quarterback afforded an estate with all this room and a lap pool in his master suite.

Mac was and had always been single. He didn't spend money wooing a woman or starting a family. He invested most of his salary from his first few years of playing in the NFL. He got good advice from his agent and invested in tech companies. He saved what he didn't invest, and suddenly, this type of home, the multi-million-dollar type, was well within his price range.

Mac stood by his choices in life. He was the cousin who had done well for himself and now lived in a mansion on the west coast where everyone wanted to come visit. His life was full. He wasn't against getting married and starting a family, but he had intentionally focused on work, and he chose to remain single all these years because of that.

Mac knew he wouldn't be able to compete at the same level professionally if he made room in his life for a relationship. He depended on himself to stay extremely disciplined and in shape during the off-season. He stayed sharp and worked hard, which was why he was currently headed to the gym.

Justin was a driven player as well. He was young—going into his second year in the league, and he was obsessed with getting better. He was a good roommate for Mac. They would motivate each other.

All this to say, Mac's work was very important to him and his status of being a single person was completely intentional. He went on dates now and then to keep his family from asking questions. But he hadn't met anyone who was worth trading all this. Not even close.

He just explained that to his sister, Katie, when she came into the room, telling him about this woman she worked with named Gretchen.

"It's not that I'm trying to be single the rest of my life, but I still have some years ahead of me with football, and I just don't think I can spare the time. I just can't afford to lose focus."

"Staying focused… big surprise from the guy who's drinking grass through a straw."

Mac smiled at his sister. She had been the one to buy the smoothie mix that was in the freezer. "Thank you for this, by the way," Mac said.

"You're not getting me to quit telling you about Gretchen. She's from Texas. San Antonio. I know we talk about going back to Galveston one day, and she's from there… she's really pretty, too. She's my age, and we get along so well."

"No thanks."

"Maaaac, I didn't even mention her for the first month because I was making sure she was worth mentioning. She's awesome."

Mac smiled at his sister and shook his head. "I cannot believe you didn't get through two months without trying to marry me off, Katie. You, of all people."

"What's that supposed to mean, me of all people?"

"You're not that much younger than me."

"Five years," Katie said, defensively.

"That's nothing."

"Yeah, but I dated Colton for two years."

"Oh, so that makes it different?" he asked, smiling at Katie.

She shrugged innocently. "Sort of," she said. "You're so afraid a woman would distract you, but some girls make guys better. I feel like I made Colton better. I tried to."

He shrugged. "Maybe. I just don't see myself getting close to any of the girls I've ever met."

"Well Mac, I don't know what to tell you. I would say that you'll find somebody one day, but seeing as how you're thirty, you might not. You might just be one of those dudes who stays single."

Mac laughed and shook his head at her. "That's what I've been trying to tell you. It's not gonna happen. There's only ever been one girl who tempted me to start wasting time on women."

"Who?"

"That girl from Nebraska."

"What girl?"

"From Evan's football games. Morgan Lake. She used to live in Nebraska when her dad was working there. They moved, though. I think she lives in California now. She was married to Tyson Richardson. They had kids and everything."

"Who's Tyson Richardson?" Katie asked, wearing a look of confusion.

"He was a football player. He died last year in a car accident."

"Oh, yeah, whoa, that was him? I heard about that. It was a big deal."

"Yeah, he was a running back for the Chargers."

"It's crazy that you had a crush on a girl that ended up marrying a football player. What are the chances?"

"That she'd marry a football player?" Mac said. "Extremely high. She's around football all the time. That's how I knew her. Her dad was Uncle Evan's coach in Nebraska."

"I knew you talked about a girl when you were up there visiting Uncle Evan, but I didn't know her dad was the coach. I thought she just lived there. I was too young. I just remember her from stories."

"I was like ten or so when he graduated, so I was really young when I first met her—maybe six or seven. She was the one I was going to marry. She's the only girl I've ever thought of like that. Morgan Lake." He smiled. "But, again, I was ten."

Mac drained the rest of his smoothie and rinsed his glass.

"Morgan Richardson now, not Lake," he said, correcting himself. "I saw her a time or two over the years with football stuff. I saw her from across the room once. Then, I shook her hand in San Francisco, and we smiled, but it was... I don't think she knew who I was. She was with Tyson by that point, anyway. They had a family and everything. But, she was the one for me way back then. She had these light brown eyes, yellow almost. And a dimple on one side."

Mac spoke casually, but Katie leveled him with an intense expression. As he spoke, her eyebrows became increasingly furrowed.

"What?" Mac asked, staring at her as her face changed.

"You're talking about this woman like you saw her yesterday," Katie said.

"No, I'm not. I'm not even trying to talk about her. I was just saying she was the only girl I can remember who gave me the feeling that I would ever even want to be anyone's boyfriend."

"Whoa, Mac, you want to be her boyfriend? What's stopping you from going after her?" Katie asked. "I'm not trying to sound heartless, but if her husband died a year ago, she might be ready to, I don't know. I don't know what her story is."

"Yeah, no, I don't either. I assume she lives in San Diego still. Her dad coaches out there, so I think she would stay there."

"Oh, gaw! She is gorgeous!" Katie said. "Oh, yeah, I could see how you would—"

"What are you doing? What are you looking at?" Mac asked.

He was scowling, but Katie couldn't see him because she was staring intensely down at her phone. She smiled and swiped, and Mac got a towel wet and wiped away a little bit of protein powder that had spilled onto the counter next to the blender. He knew his sister had searched Morgan on the internet, and it made him uncomfortable just thinking about it.

"Katie, what are you looking at?"

"That woman. Morgan. She's really pretty, aww, look, that must be her little girl. Oh, my goodness, that curly hair. How precious."

"Don't look at that. Why would you do that? Did you search her? Is that my account? Can she tell you searched her?"

"Calm down, Mac, she has no idea I'm looking at… aww, she looks so sweet. She's funny, too. Some of these faces. I love it when girls don't try to be a model all the time."

"Okay, that's enough. You don't need to look at that. I don't know why you even looked her up or why we even mentioned her in the first place."

"Because you said she was your first and only true love, Mac."

Mac laughed. "I said no such thing. I said I thought she was cool when I was nine."

"You should see her now!" Katie said. She flashed her phone at Mac, but he looked the other way.

"I don't want to see her," he said. "She's got a life and a kid. That ship sailed a long time ago."

"I hate that phrase," Katie said, shaking her head. "Did you say that ship sailed?"

"Yeah," he said.

"There's nothing final about a ship sailing. If a ship sails off, it can just turn around in the water. Nana used to say that phrase, and it always bugged me."

Mac smiled and shook his head at her. "Well, however you want to say it, she's got a kid."

"So?"

"So, she's probably with someone else by now, anyway."

"Oh, that's your excuse? She's with someone else? What if she's not?"

"It doesn't matter," Mac said. "It's irrelevant by now."

"How is it irrelevant?"

"Because, Katie, even if she was single, it's not like I would ever just call her up and ask her if she remembered me from when we were kids."

CHAPTER 2

Morgan Richardson
San Diego, California

I never, ever handled the expenses in our home.

I didn't know a thing about them.

Tyson hired an accountant to take care of our investments, and I had no idea what money was where. I had no idea how much we even had.

And then Tyson was gone, and I suddenly had no income and no idea what our assets were. My dad stepped in to help me, and our accountant did his best to explain, but I had to learn a lot in a short period of time.

I was in shock when Tyson had his accident. He loved to drive fast, but he never thought anything would happen. At first, I was putting one foot in front of the other and had more bad days than good, but it got better as days, weeks, and months passed. I was sadder than I had been in my whole life, but there was a silver lining in it all. I developed a new appreciation for life, my daughter, my family, and especially God.

I didn't know God before Tyson died, but I clung to Him during that time. I found comfort and peace in my most difficult place. I couldn't say in words what happened to me, exactly, but I came out on the other side of that experience knowing that God was real and that He loved me. It was a beautiful thing at a time that could have been really dark.

It also helped that I was distracted with survival and ensuring my daughter's future. Victoria Mae Richardson was the light of my life. It had been that way since the day she was born. The two of us were inseparable. She was an adorable, precious little girl, and I knew I would do anything to protect her.

I went straight to work, learning about our investments and income and trying to think of ways to sustain myself now that I didn't have Tyson to carry on.

So far, I was making the most of it. My youngest brother moved out of my parent's house recently, so I moved back home with my little girl. I sold the house Tyson and I were in, which was paid for and worth a good deal of money. I used the money from the house to make a real estate investment—an apartment building with ten units. It was a nice enough place, and it made money every month. I also cut spending. I went from spending whatever I wanted to trimming the fat from my purchasing, and you know what, it wasn't that big of a deal. Victoria didn't know the difference.

I knew it wouldn't come to this, but in the back of my mind, it felt good to know I could make it without my parents if I needed to. I didn't mind living with them, but it felt good to have the investment making as much money as possible. I figured if things changed with my parents, Victoria and I would have a place to stay in that apartment building, but for now, we were happy living with them.

My dad coached for the San Diego Chargers. That was how I met Tyson. He was their star running back. My father wasn't happy when I fell in love with one of his players. He had a strict policy against it.

My parents had been supportive, and my dad loved Tyson, but he had definitely tried to discourage me from being with him at first. It was a whirlwind romance and we eloped, so he didn't have much say in the matter.

I can honestly say I wouldn't have done anything differently, though, even with the way things had turned out. I pressed forward, feeling like I found purpose in caring for Victoria and being an example for her.

I liked the person I was on the other side of all this. I wished there had been other ways for me to be shaped into the woman I was now, but I trusted God enough to know that there weren't. So, I was stronger now. Different. Changed. It had been a year since the accident, and Victoria was almost three. She was growing and changing and learning new things all the time.

I was staying busy, too. I poured a ton of energy into raising Victoria, but I also spent time managing our finances, which took more time now that I cared to be involved.

I also volunteered one morning a week at a local library where I read during story time. I fell backward into that commitment. I started by taking Victoria to story time every week. The librarian who normally read the books heard me as I was sitting in the corner reading quietly to Victoria before she got started, and she approached me and asked if I'd like to read for the group.

That turned into me doing it every week. I now read the story for toddler time and stayed to read for a group of older homeschoolers. Victoria stayed with me and she made friends with some of the older kids from the second group.

I didn't mind doing it, and Barbara, the librarian, certainly didn't mind having me. She appreciated the help, and she complimented me all the time about my reading ability. She always made a point of telling me how much they missed me when I couldn't make it. But I tried to be there any time I could. Tuesday mornings had become our library time and we both looked forward to it.

Victoria and I had just finished our Tuesday morning routine. We ate an early lunch at a casual chain café near the library. We each got a scoop of ice cream afterward, and we sat outside to eat it since it was a beautiful summer day.

"Take my picture," Victoria said, giving me a huge fake smile as she held up her ice cream cone. She was eating strawberry ice cream, and some of it was running down the side of the cone. I reached out to wipe at it right before it dripped, expertly catching it and folding my napkin before tucking it into my hand again.

"I don't have my phone," I said.

"Where is it?" she said in her precious, high-pitched baby voice.

"In my purse."

"Can you get it?" she said.

But she was still posing, so I began digging in my purse for it.

"Cheeeeese," she said, holding her cone right next to her face where there was ice cream touching her cheek.

"Not yet," I said in a distracted tone as I fished for my phone. It took me a few seconds to find it, and I had to smile when I looked up to find Victoria still holding steady, smiling with the cone touching her cheek.

"Looks great," I said, smiling at her as I lined up the shot with her in the middle of the screen.

But just when I went to take the picture, a notification popped up on my screen. I went to swipe it away, but an app opened, and I went straight to the mailbox where I had a direct message waiting. I sighed. I had no idea why I couldn't get notifications turned off, first of all, and second… *why could people see once you've read their messages? Was there a way to get that turned off?*

I had no idea who this Mac Klein person was and no guess as to why he was messaging me. It was probably regarding a collaboration. I had quite a few followers on social media just from being my father's daughter and Tyson's wife. I got messages on a regular basis, and most of them were spam. I exited out of the app as quickly as I could and went straight back to the camera so I could get a photo of my poor, sweet daughter who was still patiently posing.

"I'm sorry, baby, ever since I got this new phone, I… okay, I'm taking the picture!" I said, in a sweet voice, causing her to smile even bigger, if that was even possible.

I snapped a few photos in a row.

"Beautiful!" I said, smiling as I stared down at the last one.

But then, another notification came up on my screen. I let out a sigh. "Do you know how to get messages to be quiet?" I asked my daughter, swiping at it.

Victoria didn't answer. She was focused on her ice cream now that the picture had been taken. She knew my question was rhetorical. I often asked her questions she had no idea how to answer, and she always just ignored me like she was doing right now.

Facebook opened when I touched the notification, and it took me directly to the messages. The second one was much shorter and tagged at the end of the first one.

*Evan King, not Eva King. And he really loved your dad. I forgot to say that.

Had it not been for that second comment, the shorter one, I would've closed it immediately. The words *your dad* caught my eye when I started to exit out of the app, and I read the second message, which made me want to read the first.

My eyes snapped up to the top of the longer message.

Hello Morgan, my name is Mac Klein. I play football for the Seahawks. I've played against your father several times. But I first remember him from twenty years ago when he was coaching in Nebraska. My uncle, Eva King, played for him. You and I met back then. I don't know if you remember, but I saw you at some of the home games. There was a place by the end zone where we played touch football. I was a couple of years older than you, and we hung out some while my uncle was there playing for your dad. It's been a long time, but I thought of you and wanted to reach out. I also wanted to say that I was sorry to hear about Tyson. I played against him and he was a good man and a great athlete. I understand if you're busy, but I would love to hear from you sometime. I do not do social media. My cousin insisted that I created an account, and he runs it for me. I never get on here and check these messages. If you would like to reach out sometime, you can call my cell.

He included a telephone number.

I closed the phone and went into mom mode, wiping a huge smudge of ice cream off of Victoria's nose. I was absentmindedly taking motherly action while my mind raced back to the Nebraska days. I had a giant crush on a boy that would go to those games. His name was Mac. I used to name all my Ken dolls Mac because of that boy. I mentally traveled through what seemed like actual tunnels, accessing memories, and thinking of things I hadn't thought of in years.

I remembered those games of touch football. Mac would bring friends with him and they would run the show. In my memory, I caught a glimpse of his face, and I felt something of the same crush-type nervous feelings.

I wondered what he looked like now. *Was this the same guy?* I didn't even know who he was there to watch at the time. He was my friend, and we talked, but I didn't care enough about football at the time to ask him who he was there supporting. I knew it was one of my dad's players, but I didn't remember the guy's name.

I could have guessed that Mac himself would grow up to play in the pros. I remembered him being the one to watch at those little backyard-style games we played. I definitely remembered Mac. There were several times during middle school and early high school when I wished I could get in touch with him but I had no way to do it. I considered Mac my out-of-town boyfriend back then.

CHAPTER 3

I searched my mind for childhood memories of Mac Klein while my daughter was busy finishing her ice cream cone. She didn't care for the cone itself, but she still preferred to eat ice cream out of one. She licked inside of it as far as she could, which took a little while.

I watched her, and I tended to her when needed, but my mind drifted back to those interactions with Mac when I was a little girl. I thought of the things he wrote on Facebook, but I couldn't remember exactly what his message said. I wanted to read it again. I also wondered what Mac looked like now.

I normally wouldn't get out my phone while I was trying to enjoy ice cream with my daughter, but I gave in and opened the app.

"I'm going to look at something for one minute and then we'll go," I said to Victoria. "Would you please throw all of this away?" I pointed at several things that were scattered on the table. "There's a trash can right there. You might have to make a few trips. Just start with your cone."

Victoria was a quiet little girl. She didn't talk a lot, but I could read her mannerisms, and I knew she was happy to throw things away for me. She loved to be given a task. She smiled as she hopped down from the bench in search of the trash can, which was a few feet away.

I took out my phone and opened Facebook again. First, I read the message, smiling as I thought of those touch football games. There was nothing like being outside in the brisk night air with the sounds of a crowd, the announcer, and the marching band. I had current memories of those same things, but they were all NFL memories. Those little kid memories were my dad's college football days, and those games had a different feel to them.

I smiled at the flood of feelings that hit me when I thought of those games of touch football. I thought about how I was over there for hours, unsupervised, playing with the other kids. It was a fun time in my life, and I experienced nostalgic feelings when I opened Mac's Facebook page.

There wasn't much there. I scrolled through a few motivational quotes before I saw a photograph. It was Mac, I assumed, since he was dressed in a Seattle Seahawks uniform, but it was taken from the side and he had on a helmet.

I scrolled through a couple more motivational quotes before coming to another photo of Mac. He said in his message that someone was taking care of his social media, and this sure looked like it.

The second photo featured him in uniform again, but he was on the sidelines and his helmet was off.

My heart dropped, as I focused on the familiar face. I blinked and brought the phone closer to my face. Mac was covered in sweat and smiling up at the person standing in front of him. My heart actually felt a tight pang when I saw his face. He was still that same boy—that same ruddy-cheeked, smiling boy. Only now, he had grown, his face had sharpened, and he was a man.

He still had the same smile, though.

The exact same smile.

Victoria came up to me and I realized that she was done with all of the trash, even mine. She stared up at me, smiling and expecting me to notice what a good job she did.

"Wow, that was fast, thank you my sweet helper!"

She smiled at me. "You welcome," she said.

I put my phone in my pocket. "Are you ready?" I asked.

It was an hour later when I had time to think about Facebook again. Victoria laid down for a nap, so I had some quiet time. My parents were both busy during this time of day, and I did my own thing while Victoria took her nap.

I tried to be productive during that time, but on Tuesday I was usually unable to focus after my morning at the library. Usually, I ended up watching some random TV show and spacing out. (I told myself that, anyway, when I curled up on the couch with every intention of getting on the internet.)

Mac's profile was more of the same—a few motivational quotes and then a professional photograph. He rarely posted, so that pattern only repeated four or five times before I got to the complete end of all his posts. There was one photograph toward the bottom that showed a huge family. There were what must have been sixty or eighty people in the photograph. It was taken outside on the water. I zoomed in and scanned the faces, looking for Mac.

There were a dozen young, handsome men in the photograph, but I found Mac. I was able to match him to the man in the other photos.

He was still so handsome. He was built like a quarterback—thin enough to be fast, but thick enough to get hit. He was tall and broad chested. He was a trim guy and he filled out every inch of that men's extra-large shirt he was wearing. I had been married and done enough men's laundry to tell.

I had a few guys try to call me since Tyson died, but I wasn't ready to think about that. I went on a date with a friend of a friend, but it was a disaster. I stared at Mac, wondering if I was ready to think about it now. I had to remind myself that I didn't even know for sure why he was contacting me. He obviously knew about Tyson because he mentioned him in the…

I was in the middle of having that thought when something hit me like a ton of bricks.

I went back to the third or fourth picture of him—the one where I could see his face straight on. I stared at the picture, and my mind raced back to a few years ago. It was an NFL event in San Francisco, and Tyson and I had gone there with my dad. I felt like I had stared this man in the face at that event.

I had stared him in the face.

I inspected his picture on the screen and I was transported back to that banquet. I had met him there and stared straight into his eyes. I remember feeling like he looked familiar, or even like I had known him before, but I never would've guessed it was Mac from Nebraska.

My heart was racing when I put my phone down. I definitely remembered seeing him a few years ago in San Francisco. He must've known who I was because we held eye contact, I remembered that. He gave me a sincere, sweet expression, and I felt like we knew each other. That was insane. It had to be him. I had to see if it was.

I went back to the message and read it. It didn't mention San Francisco, but I knew that was him. I stared at the phone number, wondering whether or not I should text him back. I was so caught up in the moment that I forgot that he might be on the other end of this, thinking we could get romantically involved. I knew I should think twice and make sure that I didn't give him the wrong impression, but there was nothing I could do to stop myself.

I typed out a text.

Me: Hey, it's Morgan. I was happy to hear from you! Of course I remember Nebraska! I wasn't sure if I should call or text you, but I did want to say hi. I figured you can call me if you want to talk. All the best!

I read it once and pressed send, and then I instantly regretted that last, *all the best*, line.

I almost typed a second text to try to distract him, but I left it at that. I turned on the television and found a cooking show to watch. I tried to pay attention to it, but it was useless. My mind kept wandering and I couldn't sit still. I did things like straighten items on the coffee table and pick at the edge of my fingernail.

And then he called.

I had just texted the number, so I recognized it immediately.

"Hello?" I said, picking up during the third ring. I spoke quietly. Victoria was in the next room. She was sleeping soundly, but the doors were open, so I didn't speak loudly.

"Hello? I got a message from this number. This is Mac Klein."

"Yeah, hey, Mac, this is Morgan. Morgan Rich… Lake. You knew me by Morgan Lake. I'm Les Lake's daughter."

"Yeah, hey, wow. I was just talking about you the other day. What in the world are you doing texting me? How'd you get my number?"

I was silent for a few heartbeats, feeling thrown off. "I, I, uh, got it from your message. (I paused for another second.) You contacted me earlier, on Facebook," I added.

He made a sound like he started to say something but then changed his mind. "I'm so sorry," he said. "My cousin started that Facebook account for me. He lives with me while he's going to college, and he's… I'm glad you have my number, and I'm happy you called, but if someone contacted you, it wasn't… what did they say?"

"It was a message, and it just said that…" I trailed off feeling awkward and embarrassed, like I had fallen for some kind of internet scam—a prank pulled by his cousin. I felt myself blushing and had to fight the urge to hang up. "It said nothing really. That your uncle used to play for my dad, and that you remembered playing touch football with me."

"I do remember that," he said hesitantly, his deep voice sounding sincere and melting me. He cleared his throat but then continued. "And this all makes sense, actually. I think it was my sister. She and I had a conversation the other day, and I was, uh, telling her about meeting you at those games. My cousin set up that Facebook account, but my sister must have gotten a hold of it because Ozzy wouldn't… Katie, my sister, was trying to… I'm single, and she likes to try to set me up. I'm really sorry about that."

"I'm more sorry that it wasn't really you who wanted to say 'hi,'" I said with a smile in my voice. Thankfully, I sounded way more confident and casual than I felt.

"Oh, no, no, I do want to say 'hi,'" he said. "I was actually really glad you messaged me."

"Even if you didn't message me first?" I added, still smiling.

"Yes."

"No, I totally get it about your sister," I said, lightheartedly. "I have family and friends trying to set me up lately, too."

"Wh—did you?"

"Did I what?" I asked.

"Did you get set up?" he asked.

"Oh, no, I didn't. I mean, I went on a date last month, but… no. No more for a while. Dates are awkward."

"Yeah," he said. He hesitated, and I thought he was about to say more but he didn't.

"Okay," I said after a second. I used a tone of closure like I assumed he wanted to get off the phone since the whole thing had been a big misunderstanding.

CHAPTER 4

"Do you have to go right now?" Mac asked.

"N-no, not right now," I said.

"Do you remember that kid who was double-jointed?" he asked. It was a change of topic right when I thought the conversation was coming to an end, and I went with it because I didn't want to get off the phone with him.

"Barret," I said. "He could do that thing with his thumb and that other one with his shoulder."

Mac laughed. "I forgot about his thumb," he said.

"Oh, yeah, that kid was burned into my memory," I said. "He lived in Lincoln, so he was at all of the games."

"Yeah, I was just there for some of them."

"I had forgotten your uncle's name," I said.

"Evan King," he said.

"I saw that today," I said. "Your sister wrote it in the first message she sent me. She made a typo and Evan came out Eva."

Mac laughed.

"There was a second message, correcting the first, and if that wouldn't have happened, I probably wouldn't have even read the first one. I thought you were a makeup company."

"A makeup company?" he asked with a smile in his voice.

"Mac Klein," I said. "It has a ring to it."

"A makeup-y ring?" he asked, sounding disappointed and being funny.

"Kind of," I said, smiling. "And I get contacted by makeup people, you know, asking about social media stuff—spam stuff, usually. That was why I almost overlooked your message... your sister's message... the first one."

"Wow, so I have a typo to thank for you texting me?"

"Oh, you're thankful now?" I asked, teasing him.

"I never said I wasn't thankful," he said. "I didn't tell my sister to do it, but I'm not mad about it, that's for sure."

"Then you have your sister to thank," I said.

"I guess I do," he returned. "I thought about those Nebraska games when I was talking to her the other day. I remembered that time you fell and skinned your leg."

"I still have a scar from that," I said.

"Really?"

"Yeah, it's not raised or anything, but there's a patch of skin on my leg that's just slightly darker than the rest."

"Darker?" he asked.

"Yeah, why?"

"I don't know, I feel like most of my scars are lighter."

"I don't know if it was because of where it was, but no. It's not really noticeable unless you get close, though."

"That's good," he said. "You really wiped out on that one."

I laughed. "I guess I was too young to be embarrassed," I said.

"There was no reason to be embarrassed," he said. "Everybody falls. I probably had ten skinned knees for every two of yours."

I laughed again. "I only had like three skinned knees in my whole life."

"Oh, yeah then," Mac said. "I can't even tell you how many times people described me as being *all-boy* when I was growing up. I think I was always wearing some kind of bruise or scrape."

"I bet you barely even bruise now," I said.

"I don't," Mac said, laughing. "I actually don't. It takes a lot to make me bruise now."

I smiled, thinking about it. "You must be so toughened up, you're almost made of metal."

"Some mornings I feel like I am," he said.

Both of us were smiling as we spoke. It was neat to hear from Mac after it had been so long.

"So, you're playing quarterback in Seattle?"

"Backup," Mac said. "Although I started five games last season because of Tony's knee. I'm hoping it won't be like that this year."

"I don't know if you were playing quarterback when we played you," I said, trying to remember the Seahawks.

"I wasn't," he said. "I went in at the end of the game, but Tony played most of it. I've been in Seattle a long time, though. I'm going into my seventh season."

"Wow, that is just so crazy that you're a… " I hesitated, remembering the thought I had earlier. "Mac, there was a birthday party for Jed Jones. It was in—"

"San Francisco," Mac said, cutting me off.

"Yes. I think I saw you there," I said. "Do you remember that?"

"Yes, but I didn't think you recognized me."

"I didn't. I didn't put it together until I saw your message on Facebook. I stalked your page, and I put the pieces together. Wait, did you know who I was at that party?"

"Yes," Mac said.

"You did? You knew me from Nebraska? Why didn't you say anything?"

"I don't know. You were busy and I didn't want to…" he trailed off. "I didn't know if you'd remember," he said.

"Of course I'd remember," I said. "You were one of my favorite friends over there. I wish you would have said something while I was standing there staring at you. I would have hugged you and asked you how you were doing. We could have caught up with each other."

"I should have done that," he said.

"You grew up in Texas, right?" I asked, thinking back.

"Yeah. I still go back as much as I can. My family's in the Houston area. I have some in Houston, and some just south of there in a smaller city on the coast, Galveston Island."

"Oh, that's neat," I said. "I've traveled quite a bit, but Houston's one of those cities I've never been to."

"It's cool. I grew up there, but my parents are back in Galveston now. That's where I go when I go home."

"Didn't you have a famous boxer in your family?"

"Billy Castro is my great uncle."

"That's right. Does he live in Galveston?"

"Yes. He still runs a gym there, on Bank Street. Funny story, but that's one of the main reasons I bought my house."

"Why?"

"It's not the main reason," he said. "I was looking for a house, anyway. But I couldn't resist this one when I saw the address was on Bank Street."

"So, your current house is on a street called Bank?"

"Yeah. I live on Bank Street, except it's on Mercer Island. Not to be confused with my family's Bank Street on Galveston Island."

"So, basically, you didn't care for the house, but you bought it because of the address," I said.

Mac laughed. "No, I do like the house, I love it. But at the time, I thought it was too big… which is hard to believe now because I'm in the process of adding an apartment."

"Why are you doing that?"

"I have people living with me now."

"Oh really, like roommates? Or, do you have a family? Kids? I have kids. A daughter."

"I knew you and Tyson had one. I wasn't sure how many."

"Just one," I said. "Victoria's almost three. We're together all the time. She's taking a nap right now. We're staying at my parent's house for a while, so I have roommates, too. Was that what you were saying earlier, that you have roommates? Or do you have kids, too? A wife?"

I started to say more, but I kept my mouth shut. I was nervous and I knew I had been talking too much. He already mentioned being single, and I went and asked him twice about a wife.

"I do have roommates," he said. "Two of my cousins came to Seattle to go to college. They've been with me a while. They'll be going into their third year. And then recently, two others moved in. My sister got a job in Seattle, so she's with me now. And Justin Teague, a young teammate of mine is here too."

"Is he your sister's boyfriend?"

"No, please don't even say that," Mac said, stifling a laugh. "My sister is not in Seattle to meet men. She's here for work, like me."

I could tell by his tone that he was a protective older brother, and I smiled even though he couldn't see me. "I remember you having a little sister," I said. "What's her name again?"

"Katie."

"So, your sister, Katie, lives with you, along with four others?"

"Three others. Four total. Five, if you count me."

"You do have a lot of people at your house. It's a good thing you bought one that was too big."

He laughed. "It is a good thing," he said. "What's your little girl's name? You said it already."

"Victoria."

"Yeah. That's pretty. Victoria what?"

"Mae," I said. "After my grandmother."

"Victoria Mae," he said, sounding like he was trying it out. "Do you ever shorten Victoria?"

"I call her Victoria most of the time. Every once in a while, I'll call her Tory Mae. Specifically in one song. I call her Tory Mae in that one song."

"How does it go?" he asked.

I started to sing it for him, and then I realized how silly it was. "Uh, no," I said.

"Come on!" he said. "We've played hide and seek together."

I paused for a second when he said that. Hide and seek. I had played it a couple of times with Mac. But one time, the last time I ever saw him, we not only played together, we hid together. He and I hid in the same spot. I was the one who followed him. I don't know why I did that other than I wanted to be next to him. I was too young to really know what I was feeling, but I felt something. I had a crush back then, and my stomach flipped just thinking about it. *Why was he bringing up hide and seek?*

"What were we saying?" I asked, ignoring the hide-and-seek comment and all the feelings it gave me.

"The song," he said. "Tory Mae. I was asking you to sing it for me. But you don't have to. I was just playing with you."

"I can't because it's the silliest thing you've ever heard. It's just gibberish that I made up off the top of my head one day, and it stuck."

Mac was quiet for a few seconds before he said, "I won't bug you anymore, but I would love to hear it sometime."

"*Tory Mae,*
had a great day,
she laid down in the bed and said,
oh me, oh my,
I'm ti-i-ired."

I sang it the way I always sang it to Victoria. I paused for a second afterward, but before he could speak I said, "See?"

"See what? I loved it," he said. "I didn't think it was over. I was waiting to hear the gibberish. Everything you said made total sense."

I laughed at that. "Thanks," I said.

"Was that the whole song?" he asked.

"That was all for that one," I said. "But I have a few of those little songs that I sing to her for different things."

"My mom used to sing to me, too," Mac said. "It makes me know you're a good mom, because I have the best mom, and she did that same thing."

"What'd she sing?" I asked.

"We had hedgehogs as pets when I was little, and she had a couple of songs about them. There was also one about getting on the boat because we lived on the water and did that all the time."

"You had hedgehogs?" I asked, getting stuck on that fact.

"Yes."

"As pets?" I asked.

"Yes."

"Seriously? That's crazy. Where would you even get a hedgehog? I didn't know you could just buy one. I would've loved a hedgehog. That would have been my dream pet. I was obsessed with hedgehogs."

Mac laughed. "That's a funny thing to be obsessed with," he said. "How did you get obsessed with hedgehogs and not know that they were pets?"

"I thought they lived in a town somewhere," I said. "I used to read these children's books with a hedgehog family."

"Were they called Garden City?" Mac asked.

I smiled that he knew the name. "Yes! Did you love Garden City, too?"

"I better have," he said. "My mom wrote them."

"W-what?" I asked.

We were being jovial, so I assumed he was joking.

"My mom is Lucy Klein," Mac said. "She wrote those Garden City books."

He sounded completely serious, and I was quiet for a few long heartbeats. "Lucy Klein *did* write those," I said.

"I know," he agreed with a little laugh.

"Is that lady really your mom?" I asked, still feeling like he could be messing with me.

"Yeah, she really is. That's why we had hedgehogs in our house."

I swallowed, thinking of how many times I had read those books as a child. They even made a cartoon out of it. I was a little old for the cartoon, and Victoria was a little young, but the books were a staple in my childhood.

"Are you being serious right now?" I asked.

"Yes," Mac said, sounding certain.

"Mac, that is the coolest thing ever. I seriously loved that series. Victoria loves it, too. I read it to her. Her favorite book is *Tess Saves Christmas*. She asks me to read that one all the time. I read it to her yesterday."

"That's awesome," he said, smiling. "I'll have to tell my mom. She'll love hearing that. She's always happy when people share her books with their kids."

"Oh, yes, please tell her I love those books."

"I'll tell Aunt Tess your little girl loves the Christmas book, too. She'll get a kick out of that."

"Your aunt is a hedgehog?" I asked, causing Mac to laugh.

"No, I have a real Aunt Tess. My great Aunt. She's my grandma's sister. That's where my mom got the name. She's Uncle Billy's wife."

"Bill—oh yeah, you mean Billy Castro?"

"Yes."

"So, the boxer's wife is your aunt, who is also the hedgehog."

"Yes, exactly," Mac said, smiling. "You're finally catching on." I could hear that he was in a good mood, and I was too.

"Please tell your family how much we read those books," I said, being more serious. "Garden City, huh? That is the coolest thing ever, Mac. I wish I would've known about that when we were kids. I would have loved to meet your mom. I would have asked her to autograph a book."

CHAPTER 5

"So, we went and got it x-rayed, and sure enough, it was fractured. She had to wear a little cast on it and everything."

"Poor thing," Mac said. "I've had a lot of injuries over the years, but never a broken leg."

"I know. I've never had a broken leg either. She was so tough about it. I was proud of—"

I paused mid-sentence and blinked toward the other side of the room when I saw Victoria come out of the bedroom wiping her eyes and looking sleepy.

"Hang on," I whispered to Mac. I held the phone away from my ear, blocking it. "No, baby, it's not time yet. You need to get back in there and finish your nap."

I wanted to get Victoria back to sleep as soon as possible so I could finish the conversation with Mac. I was having such a good time talking to him. I glanced at the phone as I went to get off of the couch to put her back to bed. Feeling confused, I put the phone to my ear and spoke quietly.

"Is it four o'clock?" I asked Mac, completely shocked.

"Yeah," he said.

"Oh, my goodness, I had no idea. I have to go. I'm sorry for keeping you that long." I walked over to Victoria as I held the phone to my ear. "My little girl woke up," I explained. "She took a looong nap." I hugged her and we walked to the couch together—her holding onto my leg. Victoria almost never took three-hour naps, but it was overcast outside and I had been busy talking so I hadn't been in and out of her bedroom. I couldn't believe that I had been talking to Mac that whole time. It felt like five minutes.

"I am so sorry I kept you so long," I said to Mac, wrapping it up.

"I'm not sorry," Mac said. "I'm glad I talked to you, Morgan. I had fun."

"Me too," I said. I paused, not knowing what to say next. I stared at the side of my daughter's sleepy face. I had sat down on the couch, and she was standing on her feet, but her body was collapsed onto my lap. She blinked and stared quietly at the space in front of her as she slowly woke up. I rubbed her back.

"I hope your showing goes well," Mac said.

"Me too," I said. (I had an appointment to meet a prospective tenant for an empty unit in my apartment building.) "The lady seemed nice on the phone. I hope it works out with her. It's only the second one of these I've had to do, so I'm not that good at it yet."

"I don't know why you're doing it by yourself," he said. "You could get a management company to help you with that step."

"I know, but then I would have to pay them to do it, and I don't mind. At least for now. Maybe if I buy more property some time, I'll feel differently. But I kind of like knowing what goes into it. I was in the dark for so long with taking care of my finances because I had my dad helping me, and then Tyson."

"All right, well, I didn't want you to meet anyone sketchy, but you know what you're doing," Mac said.

"Yeah, they have to fill out an application and everything," I said. "It's got a background check. I'm meeting a lady and I already have all kinds of information on her."

"Good job," he said. I could hear Mac's smile. I desperately wanted to see it. I had looked at his picture a time or two while we were talking.

"I'll be fine," I assured him. "My mom's watching Victoria while I go over there. It's only like ten minutes from here."

"You could always let me know how it goes," Mac said.

I couldn't tell if he was joking or not, but I said, "Okay. I'll text you later and let you know how it went."

"Thank you," he said, sounding a little surprised that I agreed so easily.

"I'll text you later tonight, if that's okay," I said, confirming.

"It's, yeah, it's okay. It's good."

I paused for a second, but it had been hours and I needed to end the call. "Okay, bye, Mac."

"Bye," he said slowly.

I was smiling as I went to hang up the phone.

"Who's Mac?" Victoria said sleepily.

"He's my friend from when I was a little girl."

She repeated my sentence as a question. "He's your friend from when you was a little girl?" But she was sleepy and she talked like a baby, so it came out extremely precious but almost unintelligible. I wouldn't have known what she was saying if she wouldn't have been repeating my sentence. I smiled at the sound of it.

"Yup. We were friends back when Papa was coaching football in Nebraska."

"Nebraska?" she asked, having no idea what that meant.

"Yes," I said. "It's a different state. Right now, we live on the edge of the country, and that place is in the middle. I used to live there with Papa and Grandma when I was a little girl. They have a lot of corn over there."

I made a face after I said that last statement because I wasn't quite sure if it was true since we lived in the city. The name of the team was the Cornhuskers, so I thought that must mean there was a lot of corn in Nebraska. (Although my father's NFL team had plans to relocate to Los Angeles soon, so maybe the Cornhuskers hadn't always been in Nebraska.) I didn't bother telling Victoria that I wasn't sure. I figured she wasn't really paying attention to what I was saying, anyway.

"Why do we live on the edge?" she asked. "You said we live on the edge." She smiled and shook her head like I must be joking. "But we don't, silly."

"No, you're right. We don't live on the edge of anything. I shouldn't have said it like that. I'll show you what I'm talking about on the map sometime. I just meant we live closer to the ocean now than we did back then. It's not on the edge of anything."

"Yeah," she said, calmly agreeing.

I had to smile at her.

"I was wondering where you girls were," my mom said, coming into the den where we were sitting. "I thought you had that appointment at the apartment."

"I do," I said. "I'm leaving soon."

"Did she just wake up?" Mom asked noticing that Victoria was in my lap.

Victoria, who had time to wake up by now, sprang up and shot up, standing straight as an arrow, causing my mom to laugh exaggeratedly, which made Victoria laugh. She was a quiet little girl, but every once in a while, she would do something silly like that, and she always loved it when we reacted, which was every time.

"I guess she's awake now!" My mom said, gazing at Victoria with wide eyes like she was amazed.

"I think I might eat a snack before I go to the apartments. Do you want a snack?" I asked Victoria, knowing she always did at this time.

She nodded and we all started walking toward the kitchen.

"I just found out that I sort of know the author of the Garden City hedgehog books," I said to my mom.

"How? Those have been out a long time."

She and I walked toward the kitchen, following Victoria, who scurried in front of us.

"It's the lady's son who I know," I said. "I have met her, though. A couple of times. I was a little kid. I didn't know who she was. He never told me back then that his mom wrote books."

"What? Who are you talking about?"

"A guy named Mac Klein. I knew him from Nebraska. He's from Texas, but he's in Seattle now. His parents are in Texas. His dad's a judge and his mom writes books, obviously."

"If his mom is Lucy Klein, she did that book that they just made into a movie. The one about the shipwreck. That's the same lady who did those hedgehog books. I heard Denise talking about it, she said her daughters went to that movie the day it came out."

I stared at my mom, trying to keep up. "Mom, I didn't know that was the same lady. I heard of the Lox Island movie, but I didn't realize Lucy Klein wrote that. That's crazy. Mac didn't even mention it. We talked about her Garden City books, but he never mentioned that movie. I can't believe it because we talked for three hours just now."

We were all in the kitchen by this time. Victoria was at the fridge waiting for us to open the door.

"Three hours?" my mom said at my back as I opened the door. "Who is this guy, Mac, and why would you talk to him for three hours?"

"He's a boy I used to know when Dad was coaching at Nebraska. I met him when we were little kids, and we just got in touch again."

"How?" she asked. "How old is he?"

I knew that Victoria wanted an apple, so I took one from the fridge and started to cut it. Victoria went to my mother, who picked her up and set her on the counter so she could watch me.

"He's pretty much my age. A little older—not much. He got in touch on Facebook, and then we talked on the phone."

My mom gave me a skeptical look. "I've heard of bad things happening like that, Morgan."

"What's that supposed to mean?" I asked her.

Victoria just kept quiet, watching me cut the apple.

"You have to be careful who you talk to on there," she said. "I've heard of bad things happening. If you didn't see his face, you don't even know if he's the same guy on the Facebook profile. People do that, you know. Fake accounts."

"Mom, you need to stop watching Dr. Phil," I said smiling. "It was Mac I talked to. I know him. We're friends. We talked about things that happened in Nebraska—things we both remember. He plays football."

"For a job?" she asked.

"Yes," I said, laughing. "Over in Seattle."

"The Seahawks?" she asked, sounding shocked.

I nodded, handing Victoria a slice of apple. "Yes."

"What'd you say his name was?" Mom asked.

"Mac Klein. He's a quarterback. He plays second string, and he's comfortable there."

"Like Bradley," Mom said, talking about a guy who used to play for my dad years ago in St. Louis.

"Mac and I talked about Bradley," I said, nodding. "They know each other."

"What's his name again? Mac what?" she asked.

"Klein."

"I think he was playing one time when we played Seattle," she said nodding absentmindedly. "I think he's good, too, if I remember right."

"His uncle used to play for Dad in Nebraska," I said. "That's how I met him. He came to some of the games. You met him too, but he was probably just a kid to you back then."

"Yeah you ran around with a lot of different boys and girls," Mom said. "Who was his uncle?" she added.

"Evan King," I said, smiling when I remembered Katie and that typo.

"Oh, I remember sweet Evan King," she said. "He was a little scrawny little boy from Texas when he came in, and I just watched him blossom. His mom wrote the coaching staff a letter before he came there, begging them to see his potential. I remember that, and I remember your dad taking a special interest in Evan."

"Well, that's Mac's uncle," I said.

I turned and offered my daughter the plate of perfectly sliced apples. She smiled and thanked me in her quiet voice.

"You're welcome," I said before looking at my mom.

She took a second to think while she stared blankly at the counter. She glanced at me. "So, was it Evan's mom who wrote Lox Island?" she asked, trying to put the pieces together.

"No. It was Mac's mom. Evan's sister."

"What's supposed to come of a three-hour conversation with this guy?" she asked.

I gave her a defensive glare. "What do you mean?"

"I mean, it's not like you'll ever see him. We don't even play Seattle this year. Not in the regular season, at least. Unless I'm… no, I don't remember seeing Seattle on our schedule."

"Mom, I'm not worried about the football schedule," I said. "I don't know why we talked so long, honestly. I didn't even mean to stay on the phone that long. And we just hung up, right when Victoria woke up, so I haven't even had the chance to think about it yet."

Chapter 6

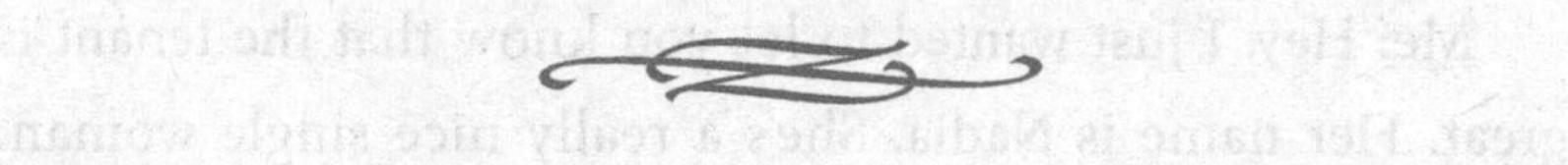

My afternoon passed in such a blur that it seemed like I was in a dream when I got back from the meeting with my tenant.

Victoria was playing with a six-year-old neighbor girl who loved to play with babies and came over all the time. They were busy playing pretend when I got home.

I talked to my mom for a couple of minutes. I thanked her for watching Victoria and told her I'd see to something simple for dinner for all of us. But she and my dad already had dinner plans.

Soon, my mom walked out of the room, and I was left with the girls who were playing with toys and going back and forth between the den and the hallway.

I took a second to put away my things and get settled. I had paperwork to deal with regarding my new tenant, and I went into my room and set everything on my desk so that I would know right where it was when I decided to tend to it.

I took care of the things I needed to do. I even went to the kitchen and started dinner. But the whole time, I had to fight the urge to get out my phone and text Mac. It was a while later, when the pasta was boiling and the fish sticks were in the oven that I gave in to the temptation. I picked up my phone, trying to hold back a smile as I composed a text.

Me: Hey, I just wanted to let you know that the tenant is great. Her name is Nadia. She's a really nice single woman. Kind of a hippie. (Insert peace sign and smiley face emojis.) I had fun catching up today. Don't be a stranger.

I read the message and then I deleted that last line about not being a stranger. I read it again and then I pressed send before I could overthink it.

I shouldn't be nervous. It was just a text, after all. I knew it was no big deal, and I had no idea why my heart sped up while I was waiting or why it began pounding seconds later when I saw my screen light up. I picked up my phone and stared at it.

Mac: I'm glad to hear that. I was wondering how it went. Thank you for letting me know. Is she staying for a year?

I smiled when I read the last line because it was a question. He wanted a response. *Why did it make me excited that he wanted a response?* I typed my answer, still smiling.

Me: Yes, she signed for a year. She's moving in on the twentieth. Also, we did all that talking today and you didn't tell me your mom wrote that movie, Lox Island. I'll have to go see it.

I hit send before I even reread it, and seconds later, I got a response from him.

Mac: Can I call you?

Instead of texting a response, I called him.

"Hey," he said, picking up. "Thank you. I'm driving, so it was hard to text."

"Oh, I'm sorry."

"No, it's fine. I was at a light, but it turned green and I didn't want to leave you hanging."

"Okay, well, if you're busy, we can hang up, I just wanted to tell you that the meeting went well today."

"I don't need to hang up, I just couldn't text. I'm on my way home. I'm glad your tenant turned out good. I was thinking about that."

"Yeah, she's really sweet. Her friend was with her. They were both excited about the place, saying she should hang this here and put her couch over there, and stuff like that."

"Oh, that's cool," Mac said.

"Yeah, I'm happy. But I still can't get over that your mom wrote that movie. We talked about the hedgehogs, but goodness, Mac, that's a big deal. Lox Island? That's huge."

"I know, thank you, and she's really excited about the movie. We got to go to the screening. It was really good. They did a great job."

"That is the coolest thing ever," I said. "Tell your mom I said congratulations. I mean, I guess she's kind of used to it, because of the cartoons or whatever, but a movie's a big deal. Is it the first time she had a movie made?"

"It is," Mac said. "And she's really excited about it. I'll tell her you said congratulations."

"I'm going to get that book," I said. "I love to read. I'll have to read it now that I know she wrote it."

"I'm sure I can get her to send you a copy," he said.

"Oh, no, I wouldn't want her to… I'll go buy a copy. I actually already did. I was talking to my mom earlier, and I told her about your mom. She was like, *'isn't that the same lady who wrote that shipwreck book?'*. Anyway, I got online and bought it already. I should have it in a couple of days."

I paused after I said it, feeling vulnerable for having told him that I talked to my mother about them. I held my breath, wondering what he would say next.

"Uh, hey, Morgan, can I call you right back? I am just pulling up at my house, and I see some people over here waiting for me."

"Of course. I'm finishing up dinner and Victoria has a little friend over here."

"What time can I call you, then? What time does she go to bed?"

"Uh, nine," I said, feeling caught off-guard. "It's usually 8:30, but she took a long nap today."

"I'll call you at nine," he said, in a little bit of a hurry.

"Okay, sounds good," I said, since I wasn't about to deny him.

We hung up the phone, and for the next three hours, I couldn't stop smiling. He was calling me back. I went in there and played pretend with the girls, stopping only long enough to tend to the food and serve our plates.

I was in a great mood. It was amazing talking to Mac and I was relieved about the tenant. It was the best day I had in a long time. I was in such a good mood that it rubbed off on the girls, and we all ended up playing and listening to music. It was like a slumber party.

And what's even better was that Mac called me at 9pm on the dot.

I was waiting for him to do it. Victoria was asleep and all of my landlord duties were done. I thought of him just before nine, so I searched the internet and looked at his picture again. I was staring at my phone when it rang.

"Hello?" I said, answering on the first ring.

"What are you doing?" he asked.

"I'm sitting here," I said. "What about you?"

"I'm at my house. Can I Facetime you?"

"Wh-uh-are you serious?"

"Yeah, why not? We haven't seen each other in twenty years. I don't do Facebook and all that."

"I have no makeup on."

"I don't either," Mac said, being serious.

I laughed. "I'm serious, Mac. How are you talking about Facetiming me right now? I'm in my pajamas, and my hair is a mess."

"We don't have to," he said easily. "I just wanted to see your face."

I paused. "Okay," I said in a resolved tone.

"Okay what?"

"Okay, we can Facetime," I said. "Half the time I'm not wearing makeup, anyway, so you might as well see me in my natural state."

"Okay, I'm hanging up and calling you right back," he said.

"Okay, bye," I said.

I hung up, and instantly flipped my head over, shaking my hair out and running my hands through it, and doing anything I could at the last second to situate and make myself look presentable. Mac called right then, so I didn't have long.

I pressed the button, accepting the call. His screen blinked and then suddenly he showed up on it. Dark hair, dark eyes, wide smile—I was so busy taking in the similarities and the changes in his face that I didn't even worry about what I looked like. I just stared closely at the portion of the screen where I could see Mac.

"Hi," I said, smiling and watching him smile back at me. "You look exactly the same!" I added, grinning excitedly as I squinted at the screen. I felt like I wanted to cry.

"Pull back so I can see your whole face," he said.

"Oh, I'm sorry. I actually forgot that this was two-sided. I was just looking at you."

I pulled back my phone, focusing on the little screen where I showed up. Mac was dressed in regular clothes and walking around what looked like an outdoor patio. It was dark out, but he was out and dressed, and I was sitting in a house in my pajamas. I just smiled at him innocently, holding the camera so he could see my face.

"Aw, hey, Morgan," he said, smiling sweetly at me.

"Hey Mac. It's so good to see you!"

"It's so good to see you too," he said. "Hang on, I was outside with Justin. But I'm heading in."

I could see him moving, but he was holding the phone where he was in the screen. He was walking, and he glanced at the screen every now and then to make sure I was still there. I just kept quiet, waiting for him to get settled. He walked across a patio and then into the house.

"I was sitting outside with Justin," he said.

"You don't have to leave your friend," I said.

"Believe me, we see each other enough," Mac said. "He bought a truck, but he's waiting for it to come in. So, right now, I'm his ride. We're together all the time."

"When are your cousins coming back?" I asked.

"They'll be here in two days," he said. "The term isn't starting back yet, but they have to get back for their jobs."

"What are they studying again?"

"Ozzy's doing photography, and my little cousin, Bri, is a business major—although she's doing stuff with the theater, too. Ozzy wanted to come here for a certain professor, but Bri just wanted to live in Seattle and check it out up here."

"Do they like it?"

"Yeah, they do."

"Did you say they were juniors?"

"Yep. About to be."

"Whoa, was that a pool?" I asked, when I saw water flash in the background of his screen as he moved. Mac tilted his camera to the side, and sure enough, I saw a long, skinny indoor pool. "That's gorgeous," I said.

"Come over and go swimming in it," he said, smiling.

The statement was innocent enough, but I experienced a wave of some kind of sensation—desire, love, attraction, all of the above. I smiled, trying to act calm even though I wasn't. I felt drawn to Mac and it had nothing to do with his indoor pool or his famous mother. It was his smile and his demeanor. I remembered thinking he was such a cool person when we were kids, and it was the same now. I just liked him and felt comfortable talking to him.

"I would if I had a bathing suit," I said, making up a fake excuse to be playful.

"Wait, you would come here if you had a swimsuit?" he asked.

"I wish," I said. "It's more about being a thousand miles away."

"I wish we were a thousand miles away," he said.

"Are we *more than that*?" I asked, disbelieving. "I thought that was too much when I said it."

"No, I think we're like twelve or thirteen hundred miles," he said. "We're as far as you can go north and south and still be in the United States."

"That's so far," I said, feeling like I might never ever see Mac in person again. "And my mom said we're not playing you guys this year—not in the regular season."

"I like that you talked to your mom about me," he said.

I had to hold back a nervous laugh. It was unbelievable seeing him after all these years. I could see from watching his camera that he was getting settled on a couch.

"I was just talking to Justin about you," he said, smiling as he sat down.

"What'd you say to him?"

"That I love my sister for doing this."

My legs stiffened, my toes curled off-screen, and I had to bite my lip to stop a gigantic grin from covering my face.

"Justin's convinced that you just called me because of what Katie wrote. He said that you wouldn't have called if I had written that message. He told me it was something she said."

"I don't know," I said. "It was really just a typo that made me look at it. Sometimes I just glance at those DM's and assume they don't really apply to me. (I paused but then continued.) But, for what it's worth, Mac, I wish you would tell your sister 'thank you' from me. I am so happy to hear from you. I've been smiling all afternoon."

I loved our conversation from earlier. I thought of all the things we talked about and how we laughed. I felt close to Mac, like I really knew him and he really knew me. I felt like I wanted to physically curl up somewhere while I talked to him on the phone. But I sat up straight, trying to look normal and unaffected since we were on Facetime.

"You're so gorgeous," he said.

We had already gone over the fact that we were both single, but it was the first time he said anything like that. He was wearing a barely there smile as he stared at the screen, looking at me. He was handsome, even on Facetime, and that was saying something since it was impossible for me to find a good angle on myself. *How could he say that?* I could see my stretched-out Facetime reflection in the corner of the screen. I thought I looked terrible.

"You're too sweet," I said.

"I mean it, Morgan." He touched his hand to his chest. "My heart's aching over here you're so beautiful."

I could feel blood rushing to my cheeks when he said that. My whole body got hot. I glanced at my reflection on the little screen, and thankfully, the lighting was just so that it wasn't obvious that I was blushing.

I touched my own chest. "My heart's aching a little, too, Mac," I said, focusing on his face on the screen. "I was thinking about those Nebraska games and remembering how much fun we had. And I just… it made my heart happy to think about that."

We talked on the phone until midnight.

Chapter 7

Mac and I talked again the next day, and the day after that. We talked every single day for a whole week. There was no mention of relationships, nor did we feel the need to define what was going on between us. We spoke to each other like we were best friends.

He had told me he thought I was beautiful on the first day, and we had some tenderness and flirtation during that conversation, but since then, we had pulled back. There had been no talk of attraction on either of our parts. I knew he liked me and he knew I liked him, though. It was obvious that we were both excited to talk to each other every day.

I had experienced the whole idea of *time flying when you're having fun*, but that happened to me on a new level with Mac. Hours seemed like minutes when I was talking to him. That section of my day just flew by like it was almost supernatural. I felt like a joke was being played on me every time I glanced at the clock. I tried to enjoy every minute, but I was so happy and content that it felt like I wanted to slow it down, like my time with him was on fast forward.

Needless to say, I looked forward to my conversation with Mac every day. Today, I had more than a phone call to look forward to. He had asked me for my address a few days ago, and this morning, my mom told me there was a package for me in the kitchen. I half expected a letter, or maybe even some flowers, but I came into the house to find a heavy box sitting on the kitchen counter. I reached out and touched it the minute I walked up to the place where it was resting. I read the label. The address and the return address were written in gorgeous script like someone had taken time on it.

It wasn't from Mac. Klein was the name on the return address, but one glance at the word Galveston let me know that the box was from his mother—or some other member of his family. I assumed it was from Mac's mom. I carried it to the other side of the kitchen, feeling excited as I grabbed a pair of scissors and began to carefully cut the tape.

I opened the box. There was purple tissue paper, and I took off a layer of it to find an envelope with more tissue paper underneath. My name was on the envelope. I picked it up, but before I took the time to open it, I moved away the next layer of tissue paper.

Hedgehogs.

Garden City.

It was a whole set.

The hardback series from when I was a little girl. They were brand new, but they were the old style—before they went mainstream with the cartoon. These were the books I had when I was little. I don't even think I had them, actually. I think I just repetitively checked them out of the school library. My family might have owned one or two of them, but I certainly never had a perfectly stacked collection of them like this. There was something at the bottom of them, too. I pulled the heavy stack of books out of the box to find a copy of Lox Island. Lox Island was smaller and thicker, so it didn't quite match, but visually, it was a gorgeous stack of books.

I set them on the counter before opening the envelope that had my name on it. There was a note inside. I began reading at the top.

Dear Morgan,

This is my third attempt at this letter. The first one was three pages long, and the second was just a note that said *hope you enjoy* with my signature.

I am a writer, and yet I am unable to decide what to write. I can remember when my son was ten years old, he came to me and told me this big long story about Coach Lake's daughter. And then, the other day, he calls me up and starts talking to me again about Coach Lake's daughter.

My son never mentions women to me. He has only done it twice in his life. I just thought it was funny that both times, it happened to be you.

Anyway, Mac thinks highly of you and he asked that I send you a book. I was given twenty-five sets of these when I signed the book deal many years ago. I had three sets still sitting and collecting dust in the attic. I thought you might be able to give one of them a better home.

Sending love from Galveston,

Lucy Klein (Mac's mom)

The letter smelled nice, like perfume. I set it down and stared at the books again. It was a gorgeous set, and I instantly found a nice place for it on a shelf in the den. The Lox Island book went straight to my bedside. I got another copy in the mail last week, and I had already read it. It was meant for teens, but I enjoyed it so much that I put the autographed copy next to my bed in case I wanted to pick it up again. I sat it on the table and flopped onto my bed. I had on jeans and I fished my phone out of my back pocket before typing a text to Mac.

Me: I just got home to a package that your mom sent. These books are amazing! Thank you! I know we said we'd talk later tonight, but call me if you get a chance.

I hit send, and ten seconds later, my phone rang.

"Hello?" I said.

"You got the books?" Mac asked.

"Yes, and they're beautiful, Mac. She signed each one and she wrote a sweet letter."

"Good. I'm glad it got there."

"Where are you?" I asked.

"I'm at the gym."

"I'm sorry," I said.

"No, I'm not even out of my truck yet. I had just pulled up when you sent the text."

"I won't keep you, I just wanted to say thank you. I'm going to write your mom a card. I saved her address off the package. Anyway, I just wanted to thank you for telling her to do that."

"Did Victoria like them?" he asked.

"She's not here, but she's going to love them. She's with my dad. He took her to the field with him today. I wish you were in San Diego," I added. "I'd take you to lunch to thank you for these."

"How about dinner?" he asked.

"Are you planning on coming to San Diego?" I asked, being silly and knowing he was joking.

"Sure. I can try."

"Are you being serious?" I asked, cautiously feeling doubtful but really wishing he would surprise me and come here sometime.

"No," he said.

"Dang it, Mac. You had me all excited for a second."

"Would you have been excited?" he asked.

I made a scoffing sound. "Don't even," I said. "You must know how excited I would be. I'm shaking right now just thinking about it."

He let out a sigh. "Let me think about it," he said. "It's only a three-hour flight, and I have three days before I have to report to training camp."

I was quiet for several seconds, trying to contain my enthusiasm. "You seem so serious," I said calmly.

"I thought I was serious," Mac replied.

"Are you?" I asked.

"Yes."

"You would actually come here?" I asked, feeling so excited I could burst.

"Yes."

"When? For how long?"

"I'll call the airport," he said. "If I can get there tonight, I'll spend two nights. If it has to be tomorrow, then, I'll only spend one. I need to be back by Saturday night to get my stuff together for Monday."

"My heart is beating out of my chest right now," I said. "That you're even thinking about coming… I'm so excited." I paused. "Are you?"

"You sound happy," he said.

"I am happy."

"Is there a hotel close to you?"

"Oh, goodness, no, Mac, my parents have friends next door who have an extra place behind their house. My mom just mentioned it being vacant yesterday, I heard her say it to my dad. I know they'd be happy to have you stay. They love my parents, and she told my mom that Dad could use the apartment if any of the team had family in town. She said it sleeps six. It's a cool little house, I've been in it. It backs up to my parents' backyard. I can see it from my window."

"Okay, I'm definitely staying there, as long as you're sure they won't mind," he said. "I'll pay them. Hey, I'm going to sit here in my truck and see what my options are for flights. I'll text you when I'm done and let you know what I find out."

"Okay," I said.

"And please double-check with your neighbors. I don't want to intrude. Especially on such short notice."

"Please, Mac, I promise they won't mind."

"Okay, I'll look at flights and let you know," he said.

"Thank you, Mac."

"For going to see you?" he asked.

"Yes, that. And the books. I really love the books. Mostly for coming here, though. That would be crazy. Let me know what you figure out. I can help you with your ticket."

"I got it," he said. "I'll let you know."

I hung up with him knowing he did have it under control. Mac didn't tell me the exact numbers, but he had invested heavily in Netflix, and I knew that the mansion on Bank Street was well within his budget.

He loved having enough room for his family. They were close. I had seen or heard different ones in the background during the last week when I had talked to Mac. I spoke to Katie one time. I wanted to thank her for contacting me on Mac's behalf, but I was nervous and I just greeted her. More recently, she got my number from Mac and texted me about an opera theater we had in San Diego. We had a nice but brief text exchange.

I was thinking of all those things as I considered Mac coming to California. I called my mom to make sure it was okay for him to stay at the Gilberts', which it was, and then I anxiously waited to find out if he found a flight.

I decided to clean while I waited, but I had only gotten about ten minutes into it when a call came in.

"Hello?" I said.

"Hey, I have two options. Arriving tomorrow at 1pm or tonight at 10:30pm."

"Are you asking me to choose?" I asked, after a brief pause.

"Yeah. What do you think?"

"Tonight," I said. "If it's up to me, I vote tonight, for sure. Is that too hard for you to pull off?"

"No," he said. "I was up for either."

"When do you go back?"

"Saturday at 11am."

"And you'll be here tonight?"

"Yes. Well, I mean, I think so. I'll know as soon as I get a ticket. Are you sure it's okay if I just show up? Is it all right with Victoria?"

"Yes, yes, and yes, Mac. Definitely yes. I didn't think I'd get to see you before you got started with your season."

"Okay, I'm coming over," he said. I could hear the excitement in his voice. "I'll let you know once I get the ticket."

"Okay. Thank you for coming, Mac. My mom said she'd let the Gilberts know you're at the house."

"Great," he said. "Thank you for setting that up."

"You're welcome. My pleasure. I can't believe you're coming. Are we really doing this?"

"I, uh, hope so, because I have a ticket that I'm just about ready to purchase after about two more… clicks… hang on… it's thinking."

"You're buying it now?"

"Yeah, I had my iPad sitting right here." He paused and we sat there being quiet for a few seconds. "Okay," he said. "It's all done. My flight leaves at seven. It won't arrive till ten-thirty, so I'll just take a cab to your parents' house."

"No, no, please," I said. "I'll be there to pick you up. Victoria will be sleeping, so she can just stay here with my mom. I'll run to the airport, no problem. I'm a pro at the airport, believe me."

"If you don't mind," he said.

"I definitely don't," I said. "I'll be waiting at baggage claim. I'll look for your flight."

"It's Delta."

"Okay," I said. "Oh, my goodness, Mac, I'll see you soon."

Chapter 8

Mac

This was really unlike Mac.

He was passionate and fun, and even spontaneous to a certain extent, but he was an extremely driven athlete, and it was not like him to rush off to San Diego three days before training camp.

Usually, during this time, he ate a balanced diet and kept to a strict routine. He did his best to keep his body in prime shape, and travel tended to wear him out, so he always stayed in Seattle during this time.

But Morgan.

Morgan Lake. It was Richardson now, but admitting that she had a different last name reminded him that she had been married. He wrestled with being jealous over a guy who was no longer alive. He felt bad about it. But at the same time, he got jealous every time he thought about him.

Mac had wanted Morgan all this time, and it seemed as though he was finally getting his wish. They had lived their own separate lives for years, and even now, Morgan was irresistible to Mac. She mentioned going there, and it was impossible for Mac to pass the chance. In spite of training camp, he instantly agreed to go to her.

And, the thing was, he wasn't mad at himself at all. He didn't regret making plans for this trip and he didn't dread it. He was chomping at the bit to get to her. He could not wait to see her.

They had talked on the phone for countless hours. They had grown close to each other on the phone. It had only been a short time, but they had talked about everything. They shared so much that Mac wasn't sure how they would react to each other when they came face-to-face.

Romance had been left out of their conversations. They were too busy telling each other stories and getting to know each other on other levels. They were friends when they were kids. They knew their personalities clicked, even back then. But Mac knew they would connect in a different way now.

When Mac was Victoria's age, his mother was a single mother living with her parents like Morgan was now. This made Mac feel protective over both Morgan and Victoria. He had heard a lot about the little girl in their conversations. He had talked to her a little bit on the phone, and he was both excited and scared to meet her in person.

He honestly had no idea how Morgan would react to him. He was planning on tricking her at the airport, just to break the ice and be silly. Morgan knew what she was getting into with Mac, anyway. He had told her enough of his family stories to know that he was a wildcard sometimes. Mac was the oldest of all the grandkids, so he had been the instigator of his fair share of tricks and pranks over the years.

Bri was taking a theater class, and she had a wig that worked as a disguise. It was long but the style was natural and could pass for a man. Mac put on the wig with a hoodie and a fake moustache, which Bri happened to have in her actor's kit. It was a nice one, and it didn't bother him at all.

Mac put everything on before he left his house. He started to take the disguise with him and change in the airport, but he thought it might be suspicious looking and get him arrested.

He actually enjoyed wearing a moustache and long hair on the plane. They were quality products, so they were comfortable and they looked natural. It was fun for Mac to be someone else for a few hours. He didn't feel bad about it at all.

Morgan had been told enough by now to not be shocked when she realized he showed up in a disguise.

And so far, it was working.

Mac's heart began pounding the instant he saw her.

They made eye contact for the slightest of seconds before he tore his gaze from hers. He made eye contact with a fake point of interest behind Morgan and waved as if he had found his person. He gave it a second before glancing at Morgan again, but she was already looking up, staring at the escalator, scanning the people behind Mac. She had already passed him up and decided he wasn't the one.

Mac headed toward her, feeling like he was in a dream. She was like an angel, staring up at that escalator, waiting for him. He wanted to cry. Maybe that's why he had dressed up. He passed it off as a surprise, but maybe subconsciously he wanted to disguise himself because he was overwhelmed about seeing her.

He stared in awe as Morgan watched the top of the escalator, waiting for him. She was standing about twenty feet from him when he reached the bottom of the escalator. He kept his eyes on her as he circled to her side to approach her.

Morgan. She was still young and innocent. She stared upward, watching the escalator. He could sit there and watch her wait for him forever. She was beautiful, and she was staring expectantly. He could tell she was happy, and he could have stood there much longer. He didn't hesitate, though. He walked up to Morgan and tapped her on the shoulder. She had her brown hair pulled back into a ponytail.

Technically, she had brown eyes. She called them brown. But they were light, almost golden in the middle. They faded into a deep amber color at the edges. The word brown didn't do them justice. Mac had brown eyes, and they were not like this.

Mac stared into those perfect eyes the instant she looked his way. Her face was serious, and then it broke into a smile, and then it became serious again as she focused on Mac. He watched her eyes roam over his face. He saw her scan his mouth, his moustache. She continued checking him out, staring at him, scanning his face, taking him in with wide eyes. Her eyes. They were like looking into honey—honey that had a soul.

Suddenly, she scrunched up her face at him and gave him a push on the shoulder.

"You dirty dog," she said, playfully scolding him and causing him to laugh. "I stared right at you and had no idea." She craned her neck in front of him and reached out to him extending her hand like she might touch his moustache. She stopped short. "That's a fake moustache," she said. It was more of a statement than a question, but she still didn't seem too sure.

"It is," he said.

"And the hair?"

"Also fake."

"I can't believe I didn't know you," she said, scanning his appearance and smiling like she honestly couldn't believe it. She was amazed and she was genuinely happy to see him, and Mac felt like his chest might burst. He didn't know how to handle Morgan. She was like a delicate, precious jewel.

Mac had been raised in a family of huggers. He was used to going in for an embrace with people, even with his teammates, but he hesitated with Morgan.

It was because he wanted to so much. He wanted to touch her so badly that he couldn't. He just stood there, watching her react to his disguise.

"I'll leave it on until we get in the car," he said. "I don't want to get tackled in here."

"Yeah, that's probably a good idea. We wouldn't want that," she said. "I can't get over this," she added, still staring as they slowly took off walking. "You're hilarious, Mac. Did you have to wear that the whole way over here?"

"Yeah," he said. "I couldn't really change at an airport without raising eyebrows. But I liked it," he added. "It was fun being someone else. They didn't give me a hard time with my ID, either. I have a beard in that."

"Yeah, I saw some facial hair in your photos."

"I grow a beard during the season." He smiled. "It looks different with a moustache only, though."

She slowly kept walking and he stayed with her.

"And the long hair threw me way off," she said.

"I probably wanted to hide behind it a little," he said.

"You're not nervous," she said, staring at him with a narrow-eyed gaze.

They had only walked a short distance when she stopped walking and turned to him. "Do you have checked bags?" she asked.

"No, I don't," he said.

Morgan started to take off but jerkily changed her mind. She went straight into a tight hug, holding onto him and resting her head on his chest. Mac held his breath while she squeezed him. She rested the side of her face on his chest, taking a deep breath and holding onto him for several long seconds.

"Sorry, Mac," she said without looking at him.

He finally remembered to breathe when he thought about answering her. He was holding a big duffel bag, but he touched her back with his free hand. He honestly felt like he had no idea how to touch a person. He felt like he might break her. He felt a little broken himself. Mac was usually sure of himself, but with Morgan, he forgot everything.

"What in the Sam Hill would you possibly be apologizing for right now?" he said, staring at her head as she held onto him.

She laughed a little at his question. "For holding you up just now. I know you thought we were walking out."

"Morgan, that's nothing to be sorry for, believe me."

She smiled as she pulled away from him, continuing on her way through the airport.

Mac wanted to say things to her, but he was oddly flustered and couldn't get words to come out of his mouth. What he wanted to say was that he loved her. But he had to stop himself. He knew it was too early for that. He followed Morgan to her car, and she gave him the keys and told him she'd give him directions if he drove.

Mac removed the disguise as soon as he got in the car. He pulled off the moustache and wig in one swift motion. He had no idea how Morgan would react to seeing him without all that stuff on, and he felt a bit nervous. She was looking at the side of his face, and she reached out and straightened his hair, touching him and easily breaking through any tension.

Mac instinctually reached up to run his hand through his hair, and his fingers accidentally touched hers. He was cripplingly attracted to this woman, but he pretended to be normal and unaffected. "That's better," he said with a smile.

"Instant haircut," she said, smiling back at him.

Mac had this whole vision where he kissed her. He reached out for her, drew her in, and kissed her right then in the car.

But it was just in his mind. He told himself she would let it happen. He knew she would. But he didn't kiss her. He didn't tell her he loved her either. He knew they had to establish a relationship and earn trust.

Mac still desperately wanted to rush things. She was the only woman who had ever made him feel like doing that. Before, he felt like he couldn't make time for a woman in his life. It was like the thought of spending his life with a woman was forced. But with Morgan, everything felt natural. Being with her felt necessary. She was simply the one.

Mac didn't know if it worked out for everyone like it did for him, but he just knew he found the person he could see himself spending the rest of his life with. He felt like every second that he wasn't using to hold Morgan, kiss her, make her his, all those seconds were being wasted.

These moments were surreal. He thought of the feelings he had about her when they were kids, and he couldn't believe he was sitting here, in her presence all these years later, staring at a grown-up version of her. It was oddly perfect. It was as if his life had come full circle.

Morgan let out a thoughtful sigh as she sat back in the passenger's seat, and Mac started the car.

CHAPTER 9

Morgan

I remember thinking that guy with the long hair and moustache was a handsome guy, but I blew past him because I was so excited to see Mac. I wasn't the type to check out guys with any intention of dating them, but I did know what a handsome man looked like, and I actually thought Mac was handsome before I even knew it was Mac.

It was like a dream, seeing him at the airport. I was anxious about our first meeting, and I loved that he did something to trick me and take me off guard. It was fun having an excuse for my nerves and adrenaline.

Mac drove and I gave him directions. It took us twenty minutes to get back to my parent's house, and it went by so fast that I regretted taking him straight there.

"My parents are still up," I said, as we pulled into their driveway. I could tell that the television was on by a certain flashing of light that came through a window when my dad was in the living room watching it.

"My dad's definitely up," I said. "I'm sure he'll try to say 'hi' to you."

"I hope so," Mac said. "It'd be weird if he just stood there and ignored me."

I laughed.

I was almost out of my twenties.

I had been married and had a baby.

I had seen some life.

Yet I felt like I was in high school when I saw my dad standing there on the other side of the door. He was staring straight at Mac and me, looking back and forth between us. I saw him glance for any sort of connection between us, but we weren't holding hands or touching at all.

Dad reached his hand out to shake Mac's hand as he leaned back, making room for us to walk inside. I saw them shaking hands as I moved.

"Les Lake," my dad said. "Welcome to our home."

"Mac Klein," Mac said. "Thank you very much, sir."

"Come on inside," my dad said, letting the door close behind us. "I guess we've met a couple of times," he said. "On the field, and way back when your uncle Evan was playing for me in Nebraska."

"Yes sir, we sure have. I remember you and a couple of the other coaches came out to eat with all of us at that pancake place."

"I definitely remember that," Dad said. "I remember your family well. They were really nice people. You guys took us out to eat a couple of times while Evan was playing for us. How's he doing?"

"Uncle Evan? He's doing great. He's got two kids in college now."

"That's unbelievable," Dad said, shaking his head.

"Where's mom?" I asked him.

"She's coming. I hollered at her. She's about to turn in, but she wanted to come meet Mac."

I showed Mac where to temporarily put his bag and we all walked to the kitchen with my dad. Mac and my father stood on adjacent sides of the room. I was planning on going to stand next to Mac, but before I went there, I made us both a glass of water. My father and Mac had an exchange about the head coach at Seattle. My dad had already done his research on Mac before he ever knew he was coming over.

"I appreciate you having me over at the last minute," Mac said. "Our camp starts next week, so I had to get the trip in now if I wanted to make it happen before the season."

"Yeah, we're training with the rookies right now," Dad said.

"Us too," Mac said. "My roommate's been at camp for two weeks. He's in his second year, but he's working with the new guys."

"Morgan was telling me you had Justin Teague staying with you."

"Yes sir, he's a good guy."

"He better be, at those prices," Dad said, causing them both to laugh.

"He is," Mac said. "Salt of the earth kind of guy. You know I wouldn't let just anyone stay at my house."

"Yeah, me neither," Dad said, joking and referring to the fact that Mac was over.

My mom came out a few seconds later, and for the next half-hour, they asked Mac questions, and he answered them. He was such a good sport about everything. He seemed like he was having a nice time talking to my parents and not just like he was tolerating them. We stood a few feet apart, but we didn't make any contact. He glanced at me while he was talking to my parents, and we smiled at each other.

It was good that my parents were there to serve as a distraction. As it stood, I got to stay quiet and get used to the idea of seeing him in person while I watched him interact with my parents.

There was a young, handsome, available man in my house. I knew him intensely and yet I hardly knew him at all. I could see the boyish features underneath that masculine face, and I knew Mac had been in my heart, even since way back then.

I was able to see his face more clearly inside my parents' house than I was in the car. I watched him, studied his face, as he interacted with my parents. *Was it too early to be in love? Because I was in love.* I was completely comfortable with Mac. I wanted to stand beside him every second and have him hold onto me.

And just like that, my parents excused themselves to head to bed. I told them we would be up for a while.

My mom stopped in the hallway on their way out. "Oh, Morgan, come look at these earrings for me if you don't mind."

I told Mac I'd be right back, and I jogged to the hallway to meet my mother. My dad had already gone ahead of us into the bedroom, and Mom stopped at the end of the hallway where we were out of sight of my father and Mac.

Her eyes were wide and she stared at me with an intense expression.

"What?" I asked. "What did you need me to look at?"

"Morgan, that boy is wonderful," she said, looking intense.

"Wh-oh Mac? I know."

"Aw, baby, he's so good-looking. And he's such a sweetheart. How in heaven's name is he still single?"

"I don't know, Mom, don't make me worry about it."

"It's nothing to worry about," she said. "He's amazing. I love him to death, Morgan!"

"Thank you, Mom," I said. "Thanks for letting me know that." I was glad she liked Mac, but goodness, I already wanted him enough as it was.

"Your dad loves him, too," she added. "I knew he was going to after he talked to Coach Simms over at Seattle." She peered toward the kitchen, being quiet, listening for Mac. "I just wanted you to know I love him," she said, still staring that way as she whispered. "I know you two are just now getting to know each other and everything, and I'm not trying to rush you..." she trailed off but then widened her eyes as she continued, "But he's amazing."

"Bridgette Anne Lake," I whispered to my mom. "I already like him."

"I'm sorry. I should really think twice before encouraging you since he's in Seattle. Forget what I said. Or not. I love you. Enjoy your time with your friend. Have fun, sweetheart."

"Thanks, Mom, I know he's great, thank you. And thanks for watching Victoria tomorrow night."

"Okay, you're welcome. We'll have fun. She and I will have a girls' night. I have plans with Hope and Nanette in the afternoon, but you can plan on me watching her after five."

"Thank you," I said.

I could not believe my mother had pulled me back there to tell me she liked Mac. I seriously thought she had to tell me something about earrings, and I walked back out to the living room smiling at her. Mac was standing in the kitchen where I had left him, and I walked that way.

It was the first time we had been in a room alone. We were in my car together, and at the airport, but those didn't count.

Mac was so handsome that I couldn't help but feel a little self-conscious around him. He had on dark, fitted jeans and a baby blue t-shirt that hugged his broad chest. He had a hoodie on at the airport, but he had shed that before we came into my parents' house. His hair was pushed away from his face, and he had his legs crossed as he leaned casually against the kitchen counter. Then he straightened and came toward me as I walked his way. Both of us were staring at each other as we converged.

"Sorry about that," I said, talking about my parents.

"Don't be," he said, smiling. "It was painless."

"I'll walk you over to the Gilberts' in a little while," I said.

"Oh, I can find my way over there if you tell me where it is."

"I'll walk you over," I said. "But we can hang out here for a while if you want."

I came to stand close to him, swaying slightly as I looked up. I tilted my head, waiting to hear his answer.

"What did you say?" he asked, realizing that it was his turn to talk.

"I said we can hang out here if you want—just in the living room or whatever. That way I can listen for Victoria. She won't wake up. She never does."

"I want to hang out wherever you are," he said. "I don't care what we do."

"Are you hungry?" I asked, "I could make you something. to eat."

"I ate on my way out," he said. "Thank you, though."

"Would you like a cup of… tea?"

"Sure," he said, smiling at me like he didn't know if I was serious or not because of how I said it. "I know you like tea, but I can't tell if you're really offering to make some."

"I was actually offering," I said, nodding.

"I'll take some tea," Mac said.

I made a cup of tea for both of us, and we drank it, talking about tea and other British things which led us to talk about music which led me to turn some on. My parents had a nice sound system in the living room, and I played music that was loud enough for us to hear but not so loud that it would disturb anyone else. There were music stations on the television and the whole thing was connected to the speakers.

I stopped on a channel when I liked the sound of a song. Indie Folk Rock, whatever that was, was the genre I had chosen. I switched the television to fireplace mode, and threw the remote onto the end of the couch.

Mac and I sat on the couch and talked for hours. He didn't touch me once, and I didn't touch him. I ached to do it, but I didn't. We talked, and we got along like we were best friends. I laughed at his jokes, and it wasn't because I was being nice, it was because he was funny. He was quick and kind, and we got along like we had known each other our whole lives.

It was different with Mac than it had been with anyone else, ever. I loved Tyson, but even with him, things had been different. I connected with Mac in a natural, unadulterated way that I had never connected with anyone else. I was one hundred percent myself with him. I looked into his eyes, and I could tell we were telling each other the truth.

I got the feeling, as we sat on that couch, that neither of us would be able to muster up the nerve to touch each other. We had accidentally bumped into each other a few times on the couch, but it was always really fleeting, and we were both a little jumpy about it. Neither of us knew where to begin.

Thankfully, we weren't awkward about it at all. We went on with our conversation, talking and catching up, telling each other everything.

It was 2am when I walked him to the Gilberts' guest house. Victoria would be up at seven, but I would tell her to go with my dad, which would buy me another hour.

"I'll be up by eight," I said to Mac as we walked across my parents' yard, headed for the neighbor's. "You don't need to get up that early," I added. "But come over anytime you're ready. I mean, even if it's tonight and you're just uncomfortable over there. You can always come back over to our house."

"I'm sure I'll be quite comfortable," he said. "And I'll wait till after eight to come over. I'll probably make it nine or ten just to give you time to sleep in."

"If I'm choosing between those two times, I'd choose nine," I said.

Mac smiled at me as we walked. He was carrying his oversized canvas duffel—the same one he had, no doubt, strapped over his shoulder many times on road trips for games.

"I'll walk over at nine, then," he said.

"I'll have Victoria with me during the day, but my mom offered to watch her tomorrow evening so that we could, you know, in case we wanted to go on a… go out to eat or something. My dad has a barbeque dinner with the team, but we don't have to do that. We can see a movie, or some live music, or whatever you want to do. We could make plans tomorrow night."

"Are you asking me out on a date right now?" Mac asked, smiling at me.

I glanced at him, hesitating as we approached the Gilberts' yard. "I think I am," I said.

CHAPTER 10

"I'll walk you to the house," I said, crossing into the neighbor's yard with Mac even though I expected to stay on my parent's side. "It's right over here," I said.

"Oh, a pool," he said as we rounded the corner.

"Yeah, feel free to use that," I offered. "That's the pool where I taught Victoria how to swim."

He nodded. "I didn't realize it was the same neighbor."

"It is, and their pool is really nice. If I didn't have to be up in a few hours, I might join you, but I have to go to bed."

"I'm tired, too," Mac said as we walked. "Maybe tomorrow."

"Yeah, that's a good idea," I said.

"The lights are on," Mac said as we got closer to the guesthouse.

"I turned them on," I said. "I came back here and checked it out before I went to get you at the airport."

We made our way to the door. He opened it, but I stayed outside. Mac peeked in. He grinned and took his bag off of his shoulder, tossing it gently onto the floor inside.

"You've walked me to my door," he said. "Now this doesn't feel right. I'm going to have to walk you back to your house."

"No, no, believe me, I know the way," I said. "It's late. I'll just run back over there."

"Okay," he said.

I leaned over and looked over my shoulder, craning my neck and looking toward my parents' house. "You can see my bedroom from here," I said. "If you give me one minute to run back over there, you'll be able to see me from that window. I'll flash the light a few times so you'll know I made it back. It's that window right there, next to that tree."

I leaned and pointed straight at the window on the second-story corner of my parent's house. Mac leaned toward me, trying to see where I was indicating. He crowded my space, and I didn't flinch. I stayed right where I was, wanting him to touch me.

"Is it the one closest to the corner?" he asked.

He smelled nice. I had been close to him quite a bit since I picked him up, but his scent was subtle enough that I had to get this close to pick up on it. It was woodsy and masculine, and I found it irresistible. I had been aching to get near him all night.

His arm came out, and he pointed toward the house. "That one?" he asked. But he was so close to me that I felt his body heat.

"Yes," I said. Before he could pull his arm away, I touched it. I reached out and grabbed it because I couldn't resist. It was lined with muscles, and I found that it was impossible not to reach out and see what it felt like.

Mac looked at me when I touched his arm. He had leaned toward me when he was pointing at the house, so his face was only a foot or two away from mine now. I was hooked. I looked up and blinked at him. We regarded each other as my hand rested on his arm. I felt like I might actually catch on fire where my hand touched him. My blood was pumping, hot and heavy in my veins. I felt the pulsing of it. I glanced at his face, at his mouth, at the perfect indention under his nose. My eyes met his again, and they were so dark, it seemed as though they were bottomless.

I was antsy and excited, and I said the first thing that crossed my mind. "Where'd you get that scar?" I asked.

"Which one?" he said, staring at me.

He moved, and we lowered our hands.

I went to step away from Mac, but he reached for me and kept a hold of me with a light touch on my elbow.

"The one on your chin," I said.

Mac reached up and touched his own chin at the spot with the scar. He used the hand that wasn't touching me, and we never broke contact.

"That's not that good of a story," he said.

"It's cool looking, though," I said.

"Is it?" he asked.

"What's the not-cool story?" I asked.

"I tripped over a tree root when I was like six years old. I forgot what I landed on. It might've been another root or just the ground. Either way, I had to get a few stitches."

I reached up and touched another spot under the corner of his mouth, right where his jaw met his chin. There was a short scar, about a half-inch.

"Do you have others with better stories?" I asked.

"Oh, so many," he said, smiling and talking slowly like he wasn't in a hurry to say goodnight. Thank goodness for this, honestly, because I wasn't in a hurry either. I didn't want to say goodnight until he held me, kissed me. I desperately wanted him to do those things.

"Show me another one," I said. "Tell me another story."

"Well, I have a couple of nice ones on my knee from surgery. Those are big, but that's not a great story. I have a few from football, but those are less exciting, too… I got bit by a snapping turtle right here," he said, finally thinking of something he considered interesting.

He showed me a scar on his finger, and I inspected it. His hand was rough from working all the time, and my heart raced at the feel of it.

"And I got this one from getting hooked with a fishing hook one time." He showed me a place on his arm for that one. Then he lifted his arm, looking at his own elbow. "This one came from a water slide," he said, pointing at a quarter-sized mark near his elbow.

"Wow," I said.

"Then there was the time I fell out of a tree."

"Oh no."

"Yeah, the branch broke."

"What kind of scars did you get from that?" I asked.

"I had a broken arm, so I had to wear a cast. I fell on a bush, too, and scraped my side. I have few scars right here." Mac touched a spot on the right side of his body. He was an athlete and he was built like one. He had a tree trunk for a middle, and watching him touch it only made me more aware of it.

"Oh, right there? Are they visible?" I asked.

"Yeah," he said.

He picked up his shirt, making a twisting motion and inadvertently flexing as he glanced down to search for the scars. My word. That stomach.

"Look, right here, see these three lines." He used his finger to trace some scars that ran across his side at a weird angle that was basically from front to back. I imagined him falling and cutting his side at the same time that he broke his arm. I felt bad for him. I wished I could have been there to stop it.

"How old were you when that happened?"

"Young," he said. "I already had these scars by the time we met each other."

"Oh really, wow. Do you remember it happening?"

As I waited for him to answer, I stooped down and leaned in, staring at the scars intensely. Mac kept his shirt pulled up, showing me the side of his body, which was lined with muscles.

"I do remember it," he said. "Like it was yesterday. I was just sitting in that tree, without a care in the world and the limb snapped."

"Aw, I hate that," I said, imagining it. "There are four of them," I said. I reached up to gently touch a scar that was back behind the others. "I'm sorry if my hands are cold," I added, pulling back after I touched it.

"It wasn't cold at all," Mac said.

But I was already standing up, and he was already putting his shirt back down.

"I have this other one," he said. "From where I got struck by lightning."

"You got struck by *lightning*?" I asked, looking amazed. "Why wasn't that the first thing you told me? You must be kidding, right? There's no way you've been struck by lightning. You would have already told me that by now. I feel like people who get struck by lightning, that's one of the first things they say when they meet you. *Hi, my name is John, and I've been struck by lightning.*"

I was being silly, and Mack knew it. But I couldn't tell about him. "You're not being serious," I said, testing him.

Mac reached up to touch his own head. "Yeah, I have a scar right on top of my head," he said.

"You do not," I said because I could tell when he was teasing me.

"I do," he insisted, still smiling.

I knew he was lying, and I laughed as he leaned down to show me something that wasn't there. He put his head so close to me that I had to back up to get a better look at it. I touched him, bringing my hands up to gently grasp his head and hold him still so I could get a better view of his scalp. I stared at the top of his head, but it was just covered with brown hair. I used my hands to gently part it, searching for any sign of a scar.

"Is there even a scar up here at all?" I asked skeptically.

Mac stepped closer to me as he reached out and put his hand on my lower back. "Probably not," he said, moving his head and smoothly inching closer to me.

Suddenly, I was in Mac's arms. He touched me gently. His hand was on my back, and I felt closer to him than I ever had. My heart hammered, and I made a conscious effort to slow it, to calm down, to breathe evenly. It was impossible, though. Mac was Mac. He was the one and only. He was the kid I had a crush on at the football games—the one I claimed was my out-of-town boyfriend all those years ago. *How could it possibly come true now?*

I was so attracted to Mac physically that it was difficult for me to process my surroundings. I was overcome with wonder about the whole situation and I leaned forward, clinging to him like gentle magnets had drawn my body to his. I just collapsed there, my face on his chest, closing my eyes, and taking in the feel and smell of him.

"Are you okay?" he asked, not pulling away. I wrapped my arms around his midsection. We knew we liked each other, but we had not made contact—not like this. I was holding onto him firmly but gently, letting my body mold to his.

"I'm fine now," I said. "I'm good. I just kept wanting to hug you, and I never got the chance."

Mac hugged me back, and we stayed there for what must have been a full minute before I pulled back. I looked up at him. My blood was so warm. I wanted to cling to him and never let go. Mac must have seen the desperation in my eyes because he kissed me. His mouth found mine, and he kissed me, letting his lips finally touch mine.

He nudged me with his mouth, turning me, tilting me effortlessly. I wasn't expecting him to do it, but I didn't hesitate. I leaned into him, looking up, kissing him back, opening my mouth.

Finally.

Mac tightened the grip he had around my back, pulling me securely against him, leaning into the kiss. I felt the hot, silky intrusion of his tongue, and I made fists with his t-shirt in my hands, holding onto him for dear life.

Mac was a man now, and I felt his muscles tense. I felt masculinity radiating off of him. He found a gentle rhythm and kissed me deeply, letting his tongue explore my mouth for several long seconds.

Good-ness.

I was needy for him, and I made a sound of disapproval when he pulled back.

This caused him to kiss me again. He went straight into kissing me deeply and he did that for a few rhythmic heartbeats before pulling away a second time.

He loved me. He wanted me. I could tell those things by how he was looking at me and how he held me—how he kissed me. I felt aches in parts of my body that I didn't know existed. I felt aches that were unlike any aches I had ever felt before. This moment was twenty years in the making, and I felt every second of it—I felt it right to my bones.

"I'm sorry," he whispered slowly, looking down at me after that second kiss.

I was quiet for a few seconds and then I said, "What in the Uncle Sam would you be sorry for?"

Mac hesitated, and then his chest shook with laughter, and he pulled back, grinning at me. "Uncle Sam?"

"Isn't that what you said, earlier? What in the Uncle-Sam-something, right."

"Sam Hill," he said.

"Who's Sam Hill?" I asked.

"I don't know. It's just something my grandma used to say."

I shrugged. "Well, you Sam Hill don't have to be sorry you kissed me just now," I said.

A slow, easy smile spread across his perfect face, and he reached up and massaged his cheeks, trying not to smile. "I don't think that's how you use it, but you can Sam Hill say it any way you please."

I let out a little laugh, shaking my head at him. "We have to get to bed," I said.

Mac kissed me on the mouth again. "I know," he answered, sounding reluctant. He kissed me one last time—slow and lazy. "I'll see you in the morning," he added.

He pulled back just far enough for us to stare into each other's eyes. My cheeks and jaw ached and I closed my eyes as I leaned up and kissed him again. It was a quick gentle one, but I couldn't stop myself.

"Sweet dreams," I said. And before we let each other go, I added, "And thank you for coming to my house, Mac. I'm unbelievably happy you're here."

He kissed me again. It wasn't the same gentle kiss I just gave him. Mac leaned down and opened his mouth again, claiming me in a brutish, celebratory way in reaction to me telling him I was happy. It was such a hard, impatient kiss that I giggled and then grinned at him when he broke it.

This man drove me wild.

I would have done crazy things like elope with him tonight if he would ask me to. Before he came, I was wondering how things would play out between us. Our relationship had been based on getting to know each other. But he wanted more with me. Now that I was in his arms, now that I was on the other side of that kiss, I knew it. I could feel it.

"Goodnight," I said.

"Goodnight, Morgan."

"Goodnight, Mac. Sleep well. I'll flash my light in one minute. Watch my window."

"Okay, I'll watch for that," he said, grinning at me as I stepped away.

I felt shy, and I went back to him one last time, placing a quick kiss on his cheek. I smiled at him as I pulled back, making myself walk away.

"Night!" I yelled as I rounded the corner.

"Night!" he yelled back.

CHAPTER 11

Was today the same day that I had gotten Lucy Klein's books in the mail?

Was that possibly the truth?

Was Mac Klein at my neighbor's right now?

Had he just kissed me harder than I'd ever been kissed?

Was this all a dream?

I went to bed in the middle of the night, having thoughts like that. Even at 3:30 in the morning, it was difficult for me to fall asleep. I was so pumped up that I had to pray for help getting my body to turn off and get even a few hours of rest.

Victoria woke me up just after eight o'clock. My alarm was set, but it didn't go off. Maybe it wasn't set. I might have turned it off in the middle of the night. Victoria said that my parents were leaving soon and told her to come wake me up.

I pulled her into bed with me, and we snuggled for a few minutes, neither of us talking.

"Grandma said your friend was coming over here today," she said, finally.

"He is," I said. "He's already here. He's staying at Jim and Connie's, but he'll be over here in a little while."

"Is he your corn friend?"

"Yes," I said, knowing she was referring to the Nebraska thing. "But I don't call him my corn friend or anything. I just call him Mac."

"Mac?"

"Probably Mister Mac to you," I said. "Since you have to think about manners."

My parents had lived all over with my dad's job, but my mother was born in Mississippi, and she still very much believed in sirs and ma'ams.

"Does Mister Mac have some popcorn?" Victoria asked.

"I don't think so," I said, laughing at her, and shifting to touch her ribs, which made her giggle and squirm.

"What kind of corn does he have?" she asked.

She laughed because she saw that it made me laugh. It was hilarious to me that she still associated Mac with corn.

Victoria was shy—not with me or my parents, but with everyone else, especially with new people. I knew she wasn't going to say anything about corn in front of Mac because she probably wouldn't talk in front of him at all. I still thought it was funny.

"He is just a regular guy," I said. "He looks like all the guys on Papa's team. In fact, he plays on a team just like Papa's."

"The See-ahhs." She had heard me say Seahawks and was trying to remember that word, but she wasn't even close.

"It's called the Seahawks," I said, doing a better job of enunciating the word for her. "A hawk is a bird, so it's a bird that lives close to the sea—a sea-hawk," I said.

"Sea-awk," she said doing her best to match me.

"Yes," I said. "And Mac has to get back to play football in Washington. He'll only be here for one day."

We stayed quiet for another minute before deciding to get up. Victoria had always been a low-key baby who loved to snuggle up to me. She liked to play, but she didn't always have to be busy. She was content to be quiet and chill.

I knew that Mac would text me before he came over, and I didn't have a text from him, so I had time. I hopped out of bed, feeling like I was about to have the best day of my life.

I went to see my parents off and take care of breakfast for Victoria and breakfast and coffee for me.

My mom didn't say anything in front of Victoria, but she did reiterate that she thought Mac was a wonderful person. I thanked her for her vote of confidence, but I assured her I didn't need any talking into about it.

Mom left, and Victoria watched cartoons while I got dressed for the day. She was always with me, and I was always paying attention to her, teaching her things. Sometimes my parents watched her, and for a little while each day she would get distracted with a cartoon. But she was, by and large, my shadow, and I didn't mind that at all.

It was nine o'clock when I got a text from Mac asking if it was okay for him to come over. I told him to please come, and moments later, I stood at the back patio door and watched him come around the neighbor's fence.

My heart ached at the sight of him. He was wearing khaki shorts, with a casual, cotton, light-colored, button-down shirt and some sandals. He was a man who had been in the game long enough to have a good wardrobe. I didn't run into too many pro athletes who didn't dress nicely. Mac knew what looked best on him and he wore it well.

I felt the urge to run to him, but I held still. Victoria was standing next to me, and when she saw him heading toward us, she pulled on my hand. It was a familiar tug, and I reached down to pick her up, settling her on my hip before turning to look at Mac again.

But he was looking at Victoria. "Hello Miss Victoria, how are you this morning?" He was so mild-mannered and sweet that Victoria smiled and leaned toward him as he walked toward us. He came closer, and she just kept leaning. She tilted over so hard that she began to fall out of my arms.

"What are you doing?" I asked in a hurried tone as I readjusted, grabbing her, steadying her.

At that same time, Mac's big hands came around her middle. "Do you want to come see me?" he asked, taking a hold of her.

She nodded, staring straight at him. He moved, getting her settled into his arms.

"You almost fell down," I said, looking at Victoria like I was amazed because it was the last thing I expected her to do.

"Hello, there, Victoria," Mac said, smiling at her as she adjusted in his arms.

"Hello," she said.

To my utter amazement, Victoria scrunched up her face and leaned in to put her face close to his. She touched his nose, making a cutesy face like he was the baby in the situation.

"Are you the corn man?" she asked.

"The kern man?" Mac asked, repeating exactly how she said it.

"The corn man," I said, feeling dumbfounded that Victoria was actually saying these things and acting this way. That playful tone she was using was usually reserved for me. She didn't even act silly like that in front of my mom.

"Am I a corn man?" Mac asked.

"I told Victoria I met you in Nebraska," I explained. "I assumed they had a lot of corn there since the name of the team was the Cornhuskers. She just remembers me saying that."

I was blown away by the way my daughter was clinging to this man. She absolutely never warmed up to anyone this quickly.

"My momma said you don't have corn anymore."

"I don't," Mac said, looking at her regretfully. "I don't carry any around with me. But I can get you some. We can go to the store. I was going to ask what you wanted to do today. Would you like to get some corn?"

She giggled. "Some popcorn?" she asked.

"Sure," Mac said. "I love popcorn. Are we eating that for breakfast, or maybe later today?"

Victoria squinted again, putting her face by his and rubbing it back and forth—her nose to his cheek. I had never, ever, ever seen her act like this when she just met someone. She was being cute and dramatic, and the fact that she was behaving this way was even more unbelievable than the fact that Mac Klein was standing on my parents' back patio in the first place.

My arms felt empty without Victoria in them. I started to reach out for her but then they both looked content, so I decided not to. I walked inside, leading the way into my parents' house.

"What's on the agenda for today besides popcorn?" Mac asked, looking at Victoria.

"What's a genda?"

"Plans," Mac said. "I was asking what you and your mom had planned."

Victoria looked at me, and I shrugged. "We could go to the kids' museum," I offered.

Victoria's face lit up.

Mac said, "I think a kids' museum sounds fun," and her face brightened even more. She was being quiet, but she was animated in a way that had me feeling stunned. Plus, she just sat in his arms like she wanted to be held by him.

***

Victoria was stuck to Mac like glue all day.

We went to the children's museum. There were interactive exhibits, like a bubble room and a room with giant blocks that you could move around to make forts. There were a lot of people there, but the three of us were in our own little world.

Victoria took to Mac, and she wanted to be next to him which meant that Mac and I put our own physical contact on hold. We were still so new at all of this that the added dynamic of having Victoria around caused us to pull back.

I watched the two of them interact all day. Mac was a natural with children, and Victoria made herself vulnerable to him in ways that had me having deep thoughts. I wondered whether or not being vulnerable to Mac's charms was genetic. Mac seemed to have something that Victoria and I were both susceptible to. He interacted with both of us in a way that felt so natural we just treated him like he was one of us. We made ourselves dangerously exposed with Mac.

He made us laugh and act silly, and by the time we got back to the house at 4pm, my face was tired from smiling so much. Mac was planning on taking me out, so we split up, going our separate ways for an hour so we could each freshen up and get dressed.

My mind was flooded with thoughts as I took a shower and picked out a new outfit. Victoria had only taken a short nap in the car, so she was tired and being really quiet. We had a busy day, and as I went on with my routine, she sprawled out on my bed, playing with the stuffed animal Mac bought her.

I wore a simple, short sundress. I had a few summer dresses that made me feel confident, so I chose one of those. The weather was warm, and I knew it would be comfortable. I wore sandals and left my hair down, parting it to the side and letting it hang over my shoulders in natural waves that I encouraged with hairspray and a diffuser.

I tried to be calm and not get nervous, but Victoria had been such a good buffer all day that I was now overthinking the fact that it would just be Mac and me. I wondered if he was worn out from doing kid stuff all day. I worried that our day had been too much too fast.

My heart was set on things working out between us, and that was scary, seeing as how there were still so many variables. I was nervous and I wanted to say the right things. I asked God to please help my heart find rest. Deep down, I knew that if it was meant to work out, it would. But I desperately wanted it to.

It was 5:30 when Mac walked over. I knew he was on his way because he sent me a text, and I sent Victoria into the living room to let him and my mom know that I would be down in just a minute.

I stared at my reflection in the mirror for one last check before I headed out. I adjusted my hair and dabbed my lips together to freshen up my lip gloss. It had been a while since I put extra effort into my appearance to try to impress a man, and I smiled at myself for caring so much. I headed downstairs, feeling like I had a mission to make Mac love me as much as I loved him.

CHAPTER 12

Mac

Mac wore jeans and a button-down shirt. He tucked it in and wore a belt, but he rolled the sleeves a couple of times and left the collar open a little. He traveled the country with professional athletes. A certain level of hygiene and personal preparation was mandatory, so he was used to keeping up with himself and looking decent when he left the house.

But tonight was different. He must've checked himself in the mirror five times before he walked over to Morgan's parents' house. He had just seen her an hour ago, and yet he was anxious all over again. He knocked on their back door.

"Come in, Mac!" Bridgette yelled when she heard him. He opened the door and saw that little Victoria was standing next to her grandmother, looking shy. "Victoria just came down and told me to tell you Morgan would be right down," Bridgette said.

"Oh, okay, thank you," Mac said. He walked toward them.

"Les has a little cookout tonight with some of the guys from the team," Bridgette said. "It's Rodney and some of the coaches with the rookies, I think. Anyway, he wanted me to make sure you knew it's going to be casual and he'd love for you and Morgan to swing by."

"What is it?" Mac asked.

"A barbeque tonight at Rodney Chiasson's house. Morgan usually goes with him, so he told me to make sure you knew you were welcome, too. Morgan said she might skip it tonight, but she likes to go with her dad to all his football stuff."

Just then, Morgan came into the room, wearing a little white dress with gold sandals that strapped up her foot and ankle.

She might as well have been an angel.

"I talked to Dad about it," Morgan said, talking to her mom. "He mentioned it to me last week. I didn't know Mac would be here."

"Oh, don't miss it because of me," Mac said.

"No, no," both of them said at the same time.

"I was talking about you both going," Bridgette said.

And at the same time, Morgan said, "If anything, we'd both go."

"You don't have to go," Bridgette added, looking at Morgan. "I just wanted to tell you Dad mentioned it again before he left just now.

"We might," Morgan said. She stepped closer to Mac, making real eye contact with him for the first time since she came downstairs. He wanted to tell her how beautiful she was, but he hesitated in front of her mom and Victoria.

"I like your dress," he said, hoping that sounded neutral enough.

"Thanks," she replied, grabbing a piece of fabric near her thigh and performing a little back-and-forth motion to show him how it flowed.

Mac thought he might explode. She looked like a literal angel from actual heaven. And he could smell her. She smelled like a summer day. Mac tried his best to seem casual, holding an easy smile when she curtsied and modeled the dress.

"Yeah that looks nice," Bridgette said. "You know where Rodney's house is if you decide to go over there."

"Okay, thank you," Morgan said. She clapped her hands together a couple of times, looking at Victoria and making it obvious that she wanted her to come over there. Victoria went to Morgan who stooped to talk to her. "I love you so much," Morgan said.

"I love you, too," the little girl said.

"I'll probably be home after you're already sleeping," Morgan added.

"Okay."

"Go tell Mister Mac goodbye."

There was absolutely no hesitation. As soon as Morgan gave the word, Victoria left her mother and ran over to Mac who scooped her up easily.

"Have fun with your grandma," Mac said.

"I'm going to get candy," Victoria said.

"Not too much candy," Morgan said, talking to her mother as much as she was talking to Victoria.

She kissed Victoria while Mac was still holding her, and oddly enough, to Mac it was the coolest thing in the world. He loved seeing them from that perspective. It was a moment in time that he would always remember. He felt the urge to protect both of them and try to make sure they both stayed happy.

"I was thinking about that place called The Bing Room," she told her mom. "They have live music, but we won't be too late."

"Don't worry about us, we'll be fine, sweetheart. Take your time."

So, Mac and Morgan headed out for the evening. They walked slowly to the driveway, talking the whole time about their plans, or lack of them.

They chose to go to the barbecue at Rodney's house. They would drop by and see how it went. Morgan said it was an option to eat Rodney's barbeque, but they were both open to leaving the party and going to eat at a restaurant. It wasn't that they were being indecisive, but both of them were easy-going people and they were up for whatever that night.

The two of them talked on the way to Rodney's, but they didn't make physical contact. Morgan leaned toward him, and they came close to touching a few times, but it didn't happen.

She looked beautiful, and she was trying to look that way for him. Mac knew she wanted to be close to him, but it was difficult for him to reach out and touch her. The air between them was charged, but she gave him directions, and Mac acted normal. But he did not feel normal. He felt like he was about to jump out of his own skin.

There were plenty of distractions when they arrived at Rodney's house. It was more packed than Mac anticipated. It wasn't a gigantic house, so everybody was sort of crammed into different rooms. There were fifteen or twenty people in the living room and what seemed to be about as many in the kitchen.

Morgan leaned in and talked to Mac as they made their way through the house. She told Mac that there was an area outside where others had gathered and that her dad was probably out there.

"Mac-attack Klein!" Someone said Mac's name while they were walking through the living room. Mac turned and recognized the guy instantly.

Patrick Jones. He was a defensive coach who had been with Seattle for Mac's first three seasons. Mac had always liked Patrick, and it was good seeing him.

"Hey, what's up Coach Jonesy," Mac said, going in for a handshake and shoulder bump.

"What's up with me? I work here! What's up with you?" Patrick said. "Did you get traded? You with us now?"

"No, no, I'm still with Seattle," Mac said. "I start camp on Monday. I'm just here for the weekend, visiting Coach Lake and Morgan," he said, gesturing to Morgan who was standing there, smiling.

"Hey, Coach Jones," Morgan said.

"How you doin' there, sweetie?"

"I'm doing real well, thank you," she said.

"How's that little girl of yours?"

"Getting big way too fast," Morgan said.

Patrick Jones laughed. "They tend to do that," he said. "I have two and both of them have families of their own now." But he was curious about seeing Mac and he turned to talk to him. "I heard Jose Morales was coming back."

"He is," Mac said, nodding. "I'm excited to have him back. You know, he's been off for the last two years."

"I heard about that," Patrick said. "I was talking to Les about that yesterday. He was asking me about you. Hey, what's that Teague kid all about?"

"He's a good guy," Mac said, nodding. "He's actually staying with me."

"Come on, you have the room? You must still be single."

"I am," Mac said. "I have some family living with me, though. And Justin."

Suddenly, a young man rushed up to them, causing them to stop their conversation. "Coach Lake said that I should come tell you that he's outside and you should come out there."

"Thank you, Alex," Morgan said. "Tell him we'll be out there in a second." Alex nodded and turned to leave.

"How'd you meet Alex already?" Patrick asked Morgan. "I thought he just got here yesterday."

"Dad had me take a bunch of sandwiches up there yesterday when the morning practice was over. I met him then."

"Oh, yeah. Those were delicious," Patrick said. "I got one of those. Thank you for that."

"I just delivered them, but you're welcome." She smiled at him and then at Mac, reaching out to put her hand on Mac's arm. They made eye contact, and Mac felt like he could toss her over his shoulder and take her home. *Why would they come here with all these athletes while she was wearing that dress?* Mac was constantly on edge, watching to make sure nobody was looking at her.

"I'll go talk to my dad," she said, smiling. "Otherwise he'll keep sending people over here. Stay and talk to Coach Jones and just meet me outside when you're done." She was being casual, and Mac went with it, assuming that's what she wanted in front of the team.

"Okay," he said with an easy nod. "I'll be out there in a few minutes."

"So, is that big boy from Penn State shaping up to be any good?" Patrick went straight into asking Mac about football when Morgan walked away, and the two gentlemen proceeded to have a ten-minute conversation about football that would've easily been a two-hour one if Mac had let Patrick keep talking.

Mac made his way out to the back patio, but he was stopped by another NFL contact. This one, Shawn Coleman, was the younger brother of one of Mac's good friends from years ago in college. Shawn had a successful career at UCLA and now he was going into his first year on Coach Lake's team.

Mac tried his best to communicate with Shawn during their brief conversation, but he was distracted. Morgan was standing outside, and Mac could see her from his place near the glass doors. She was standing next to the swimming pool, facing mostly away from Mac. He could see the side of her jaw and face, but she was talking to a group of people and was mostly looking away from him. She had no idea he could see her.

"You're going to love Coach Lake," Mac said, continuing the conversation with Shawn as best he could while being completely distracted. Morgan was standing next to her father, and the two of them were talking to three other people. All men. All young men. All three of these young athletes were staring at Coach Lake and his daughter like they were royalty. *Who is he kidding?* They weren't staring at Coach Lake. They were staring at Morgan.

Mac was around men all the time. He knew what it looked like when they were trying to look good and impress a woman, and all three of these guys were doing it right then—one of them, especially. Even from a distance, he could see them fighting for dominance.

What was Morgan even doing here in this den of iniquity in the first place? Mac would normally find some sort of humor in those kinds of thoughts, but for now, all he could do was think about finishing this conversation with Shawn so that he could get outside to Morgan.

Shawn was excited to see Mac and asked him several direct questions. Mac was normally an engaging, friendly guy, and he didn't want to be rude, so he stood there and spoke as cordially as he could.

But it was difficult because, the whole time, he could see those guys doing their best to be alpha male in front of Morgan. One of them specifically was looking at her a lot. Mac balled his fist instinctually and he played it off in a stretching motion, smiling and stretching as he talked to Shawn.

Within another minute or two, Mac wrapped up the conversation, excused himself, and headed outside.

CHAPTER 13

Morgan

I had no idea why I left Mac's side. I could tell that Patrick Jones wanted to talk to him, and I felt like I should let them catch up.

I regretted it instantly.

I wanted him next to me, and it felt empty without him there.

I found my dad standing by the pool, talking to a few of his players. They were talking about superhero movies and which ones were their favorites.

My dad, who was obsessed with football, never watched movies. But he played along, nodding and smiling. I, on the other hand, loved superhero movies. I had my mom watch Victoria so that I could go with a friend to see the most recent Avengers movie the day it came out. I had seen all the movies the guys were talking about. It was a relief to have an easy conversation while I was regretting leaving Mac.

Ben Ruiz was the one who was into it the most. He knew all about Marvel versus DC and things that were over my head, honestly. He was in his third year as a player, but he was new to our team, and I could tell he was anxious to impress my dad.

"You're going to have to come with us to see the new Star Wars movie when it comes out," Ben said to me. "It's coming in December."

But before I had the chance to answer him, I noticed the guys looking behind my shoulder and I figured by how they were staring that someone was walking up to us. I hoped it was Mac.

It was. I smiled and turned a little and stepped back, welcoming Mac into the circle once I saw that it was him. By instinct, I reached out to touch his arm, and he reached out for me.

"Hey, there you are," I said.

For a second, we both held onto each other's arms lightly. We let go when I started the introductions.

"Mac Klein, this is Ben, Collin, and Henry. And of course, you know my dad," I said.

"Mac Klein, number eight, Seattle Seahawks," Collin said. "I knew who you were. I saw you right when you came out here." Collin stepped forward and shook Mac's hand. "I don't know how many times I've watched that last run during the game you played against the Raiders in 2012. Bro, you came in cold off the bench when Tony went down with his knee, and you were like clutch, clutch, clutch, first down, first down. I was a sophomore in college, and I remember thinking, I want to be Mac Klein one day, bro."

"Wow, thank you," Mac said smiling and shaking his hand.

"Are you playing for us now?" Collin added, looking excited.

"No, I'm still in Seattle, I'm just here, visiting with Coach Lake and Morgan."

"Aw, man, that's too bad," Collin said.

"What'd you say your name was?" Mac asked.

"Collin Connor."

"Oh, the quarterback from Iowa?"

"Yes sir." Collin looked excited about Mac knowing that.

"I've seen you play before," Mac said. "Les, you got a good one right here."

"I know we did," Les said. "Y'all ought to be scared. I got three good ones right here. Ben's in his third year. He played two seasons down in Miami."

"Okay," Mac said. He smiled at them, checking them out.

"Do we play Seattle this season?" Henry asked.

"No," Ben said. His tone was serious.

My dad went on talking about their schedule, but I was distracted by Ben. He stared at Mac with a serious expression. He wasn't nearly as impressed with Mac as Collin was. Ben was a six-foot-four safety who was known for being too fast for his size. He stood up, stretching to his full height, looking way more straight-faced than he had been when we were talking about Marvel versus DC.

I thought maybe he was a little jealous that Collin was getting all the attention, but then I realized that he was looking at Mac like he was feeling competitive with him.

This realization made me step closer to Mac. I moved toward him, glancing at him with a smile, which he returned. Our eyes stayed locked for a couple of seconds before my dad spoke to Mac again, talking about Seattle as a city.

Everybody always brought up Pike Place Market when they talked about Seattle, and Mac was prepared with a few funny stories and references to the fish-throwing. He was charming, and everyone besides Ben loved him. We didn't make contact at first, but after a few exchanges, I reached out and put my hand on his arm. I looked at him when I did that, and he gave me a smile.

We touched for a few seconds right then, and then a few minutes later, when someone else came up to our group, we touched again. Mac put his hand out to steady me when he moved, and I reached out, awkwardly taking his hand and holding onto it with my fingertips. I looked at him to make sure it was okay, and he was staring back at me like he was wondering if I was okay with it. I smiled at him, and he turned my hand and gripped it tighter. My smile broadened. I couldn't help it with all the electric feelings in my hand where we touched.

We were trying to be somewhat discreet, but we were sharing a moment. We adjusted where we could stand next to each other and hold hands and not be awkward. I was nervous about it, but Mac was confident, and the whole thing came across as natural. He held onto my hand casually like we had been standing that way for years. We held the contact as we continued talking to everyone who was standing around us.

After a while, Rodney told my dad the food was ready, and my dad gathered everyone onto the patio. He made a speech before Rodney took over, giving instructions for serving food. We shuffled around a little during this time, but Mac never lost contact with me. Our hands always found each other. Even if we had to move and got broken apart for a moment, we came together again.

Mac was known for being an outgoing, personable athlete. He had a reputation for telling jokes and stories and putting people in a good mood, and I saw it in action as he effortlessly got along with members of my dad's team. Ben was the only one who didn't click with Mac, and eventually, he stepped away and found other people to talk to.

I didn't leave Mac's side for a second. He and I decided to stay at the party and eat rather than go to a restaurant. The food smelled delicious, and there was so much of it that it almost felt wasteful to leave and go eat at a restaurant.

Just before we ate, I left Mac in the kitchen for a minute while I went to the restroom. Anytime I was away from Victoria, I checked my phone on a regular basis. I fished it out of my purse as I walked down Rodney's hallway.

I was already looking at it by the time I made it to the restroom. It was unoccupied, and I stepped inside, closing the door behind me. I gazed curiously at my screen when I saw that it was a text with a video from my mom. I clicked on it, and saw that it started with my mom staring at the camera.

"She is cracking me up!" Mom said, whispering straight at the phone camera like she was talking to me. "Your daughter. You've got to hear her, Morgan."

Then the screen shifted and got blurry and dark as she walked.

I could hear singing.

I heard some unintelligible sing-song noises in Victoria's voice. And then the camera got placed on the shelf and suddenly I could see and hear her. Victoria was holding a stuffed animal, moving around the living room, and not at all noticing the camera.

"Ohhhhhh, Mackey, Maaaa-aaa-aaaa-aaaackey! Oh, dear, I love you so much. Mackey-Mac-Mac-Maaaaaaaccckkkkeyyyyy. Oh dear. Oh dear. Oh, oh, oh, oh, dee-e-ee-ear. Maaaaac-key."

It was a dramatic serious singing voice, and she was just spacing out, enjoying the moment, thinking about her new friend, and feeling happy. She was swaying and humming, and then the video suddenly ended.

I sat there, staring at my phone.

I was already in love with Mac, and seeing my daughter like that only solidified my feelings. I went through the process of using the restroom and washing my hands, but the whole time I was smiling at the memory of that song. Just the fact that she was calling him Mackey was funny and precious to me. My heart was full, and I stared into my own eyes as I looked in the bathroom mirror.

Sometimes, for my own entertainment, I would make up a haiku. I had always liked haikus. I took comfort in their structure and in their short length. I washed my hands, thinking of one.

Last week you weren't here.

But today we can see you.

And now we sing songs.

I made it about Victoria's song because it was that which inspired my impromptu haiku, anyway.

I had washed and dried my hands by the time I finished with the haiku.

I opened the door, smiling at myself for being so in love. "Ahh," I made a little high-pitched squeal, feeling like I got caught when I opened the door and saw Mac standing right there. "I didn't expect anyone to be standing there," I said.

"Why do you have to be so beautiful, Morgan? Why were you smiling?"

"I was thinking about you, and about poetry, and I was just… songs… I was thinking about songs, too."

"You sure did a lot of thinking in there," he said, smiling.

I closed the bathroom door behind me, and Mac came a little closer, stepping toward me as I leaned back. He was wearing an unreadable but somewhat intense expression.

"What are *you* thinking?" I asked.

"I am wondering, Morgan, how in the world your father lets you hang out in places like this with these dudes ogling you all the time."

"What? They're not ogling," I said, pretending to be defensive.

Mac looked like he was serious, but I could tell he was being lighthearted. "I was dying out there," he said being more serious and, stepping even closer. "It was taking all of my strength to stop myself from… you can't tell me you didn't see the way Ben was looking at you? Even after you were standing with me, he… I was about to… I seriously do not like that guy."

CHAPTER 14

I stood in the hallway. My back was to a closed door, and Mac was standing close to me, hovering over me. I had to lean my head against the door to look up at him, and his proximity took my breath away. He had just told me he didn't like Ben for jealous reasons, and his brutish behavior, albeit lighthearted, made my heart race.

I pretended to think he was serious, and I went to him, touching his collar with my hand as I stretched toward him a few inches. We had been holding back on the contact all day, and it felt so good to just stand there and look at him with no one else around. I stared at his face.

"I should go ahead and make it clear that I do not care about Ben Ruiz or anyone else at this party," I said, trying not to sound breathless. I glanced to my right. "Excuse us," I said, noticing someone coming down the hall to use the restroom. "It's open," I said to them.

I pulled Mac further down the hall, away from the action, to a bend where we could hardly be seen. I positioned myself against the wall again before pulling him in and glancing at him with a shy smile.

"So, what I was saying is that, in the few seconds that I was in the restroom just now, I figured out that I have a little bit of a crush on you, Mac," I said it so quietly that he leaned in to listen closer to me, his body making contact with mine.

"You what?" he asked, coming closer still.

"You heard me," I said.

"Say it," he said, he leaned down and kissed me by nipping gently at my lip and then pulling back.

"I dooo," I said helplessly. "I like you, okay? There. I said it. I can't help it. You *make me* like you. I can't resist you."

"Thank goodness, Morgan," Mac said, shaking his head. "I hope you like me enough not to mess with these other guys. I don't know how I'm supposed to function in Seattle knowing every free safety on this team is trying to get you to look at him."

I laughed at Mac because he was funny—the things he said and the way he said them—he had a magnetic personality. "It's not just the free-safties who try to get me to look at them," I said, teasing him.

Mac stubbornly leaned into me like he was going to hold me captive. "I'm the one who's out there going crazy, imagining you in the locker room."

"You know as well as I do that I don't go in the locker room."

"Please don't ever go in there," he said, looking like he was aching at the thought of it.

It made me giggle that he was being so protective of me. "I won't," I said. I reached out to touch his sides as he leaned into me. He had on a dress shirt made of thin cotton, and I could easily feel the tense, tight, warm body underneath it. He leaned down and tugged at my lip again, pulling back instantly after he did it, causing me to grin at him. He leaned in again. I thought he was going to do it a third time because he used that same quick motion, but he stayed there and kissed me gently, slowly this time. I held my breath and then let it out with a sigh.

His kiss was perfect.

He let his mouth gently mold to mine before pulling back. We had just kissed, and I was aching for it to happen again. I leaned up, placing my face right next to his so we were cheek to cheek. Someone left the bathroom, and another person came in. No one paid attention to us. I assumed they didn't even see us. I couldn't really see them.

"You shouldn't worry about me looking at anyone else," I said.

"Really, why?" he whispered.

"Because all I can see is you. You're literally standing right in front of me where all I can see is you and nothing else."

I was speaking dryly, and Mac smiled, licking his lips. "What about when I'm just standing next to you?" he asked.

"Actually, I know this is going to sound cheesy even before I say it, but I do only see you, Mac. No matter where you're standing. Ever since you first contacted me, or your sister contacted me or whoever... I just can't get you off my mind. So, no, it's like, Ben who? I don't know if it's smart to tell you how I feel, or if it's going to make you feel differently about me, but there it is. I don't look at anyone the way I look at—"

I didn't finish the sentence because Mac took my hand, pressing it to his own hip. With his other hand, he held onto my lower waist, pulling me toward him as he trapped me against the wall. I could not think of a single place I'd rather be. Not a single place. The way Mac touched me... I was in paradise.

"Kiss me on the lips," he said.

I pulled back and then leaned up, kissing him.

"Not right now," he said smiling. "Although thank you. But I meant when we're out there. When we go back out. Try to find a time to kiss me on the lips while we're out there with everyone else."

I let out a little laugh at the thought of doing that. He and I had maintained light contact, but it had been discreet and often hidden. I thought of kissing him.

"Is that a request, or a dare, or what?" I asked.

"Definitely a dare," he said, looking at me like I was crazy. "Why would I request something like that? That would just be weird of me. It's definitely a dare."

"Oh, a dare?" I said. "Okay, well, in that case..." I stared at him seriously before saying, "So, I'm just supposed to lean over and kiss you some time out of nowhere?"

"Yep."

"You're not going to leave me hanging, are you? You'll kiss me back, right?"

"You know better than to ask that," he said.

"Let me try one more time, just for practice," I said. "So, you would just be out there, and I'll walk up to you, and I'll be like…"

I leaned up and kissed him once, a slow, soft, sticky one. And then I pulled back for a second before kissing him again.

"One more practice," I said before doing it a third time. I could tell that the gentle, barely there way I kissed him caused tension to grow in his body.

"We better go eat, I guess," I said.

"Yeah," he agreed, although he didn't move.

"And by the way, I'll take that dare," I said. "Unless you don't want me to do it."

"Me? Oh, I want you to," he said. "Of course I want it. I'm not the one whose dad is out there, though. In fact, I was going tell you not to do it if you feel uncomfortable in front of your dad."

"You're letting me off that easy?" I asked. "I thought I already took the dare."

"Good," he said. "Just know that I'll give you another dare and save the kissing for later when your dad's not around if you want."

I smiled at him. "I'd like the option to kiss you out there if I find the right time," I said. "But what's another dare, just in case?"

He thought about it for a second. "Say Sam Hill in front of everybody," he said.

"What?" I asked.

"The phrase from earlier," he said. "Say *what in the Sam Hill* in front of everybody out there. Just work it into the conversation somehow."

I laughed, imagining myself doing that. "What if I do both of them? What if I decide to do both dares? Are you sure you'd want to kiss the same girl who says Sam Hill? Wouldn't one dare sort of negate the other?"

"Not at all," he said, being serious even though we were half-joking about all of this. "I said Sam Hill earlier, and you still kissed me. And besides, you can act as weird as you want out there," he said. "Anything so those guys will leave you alone."

"My dad makes sure they leave me alone," I said.

The obvious comeback would be to say he hadn't done that with Tyson, but Mac didn't go there.

"Good," he said. "Because I was hurtin' out there."

"Aw, I'm sorry," I said, and I put my head on his shoulder, hugging him one last time before we broke apart and headed back toward the party.

We made our plates and ate dinner and then dessert, all while mingling with players, coaches, and my dad. We had our hands full with eating, so we didn't make obvious contact with each other, but Mac stayed close to me the whole time. He was a people person, and he had everyone who spoke to us feeling engaged and included. I was proud of him, and I caught myself smiling at him all the time, even when he was talking to other people.

We stood around the kitchen, eating dessert with my dad and about five other people. I knew we would be leaving soon. We had been there for a while, and my dad, who was always one of the first to leave, had already mentioned making his own exit.

We were finishing with our dessert, which was various pies that Rodney's mother had made. They had several to choose from—cherry, apple, lemon, and chocolate. Mac and I both ate cherry.

I knew I had to do the dare. It was getting close to time to go, and I just had to—even for my own entertainment and Mac's. My dad was standing next to us and a couple of coaches were within earshot.

I was nervous, but I took a deep breath and said. "Man, that cherry pie is good. I wonder where the Samuel Hill she got that recipe."

This was an honest mistake. The phrase was new enough to me, and I had enough nerves going that I actually thought I was correct by saying Samuel Hill instead of Sam.

My dad just stared at me, and I blinked.

"For the cherry pie," I said, trying not to crack a smile.

"I was wondering where in the Sam Hill she got it, too," Mac said easily, causing several people to laugh like they finally figured out what I was saying.

"What'd I say?" I asked.

"Samuel Hill," Mac said.

"I said Samuel Hill?" I asked, genuinely surprised.

Mac nodded.

"And it's supposed to be Sam?" I asked.

Mac smiled sweetly and nodded again.

My dad and a few other guys got a little laugh at it, and I didn't mind. I laughed too. And I figured the dare had been completed even though I used Sam's full name.

Everyone else continued talking about the pies, and I glanced at Mac.

"You're hilarious," he said to me, speaking so quietly that I knew no one else could hear.

"Did I really say Samuel?" I asked, whispering back.

"Yes."

"And it's for sure Sam?" I said.

His smile broadened. "Yes."

I had to get out of my seat a little, but I did it in a confident, quick motion. I stood up right then and planted a deliberate kiss on Mac's mouth. I just aimed for his mouth, shot in, and executed a quick kiss before sitting down again. It was fast, but he definitely kissed me back.

Mac shook his head a little. "Feeling brave," he said, wearing an amused smile and still speaking low enough that only I could hear.

A couple of people had noticed us, but I didn't care. I just shrugged. "I guess I am."

Chapter 15

We left Rodney's at the same time as my father.

Dad headed home, and Mac and I went to find something else to do. I told him about the venue that was casual and always had good bands, and Mac said that sounded like as good a plan as any.

The place was called the Bing Room. The bands playing that evening were apparently really popular because there were signs on the door saying that it was sold out.

"I've actually never been here before when it's sold out," I said, trying the door in spite of the sign.

There were people standing outside, so I knew that they were going in and out.

A flood of music hit us as the door opened.

Mac stood back and let me go in ahead of him.

"I need to see your bracelet!" A guy was standing right next to the door, and he leaned over and yelled over the music.

"What bracelet?" I asked.

"You need an armband to get in," he said, gesturing to his own wrist. "We're sold out."

He looked regretful as he showed us the plastic bracelet. It was about an inch thick, and it was marked with the name of the venue and the date. There was purple going down the center with a checkerboard pattern at the edge, and there was no way you could make a fake one.

"It's Leah and the Desert Roses tonight. We've been sold out for months. You have to have one of these to get in," he explained. "I'm sorry, but I'd get fired if I let you in without one. It's a thing with the fire marshal. If you can talk someone else into giving you theirs, then you'll be golden." He glanced at the group of people who were standing outside, but they seemed like they intended to go back in.

"I saw a few leaving earlier, and I'm sure some will be leaving after this band," he said. "You can try to get your hands on a wristband, but I can't let you in without one. I'd lose my job."

"Okay," I said, since he didn't seem like it was negotiable.

We stepped back and he closed the door, looking regretful. It was amazing in there. The band sounded like they were playing great, and the place was packed with people. I desperately wanted to go in and take Mac.

"That is too bad!" I said, looking more disappointed than I really was.

"Do you want me to ask one of these people to give you their bracelet," he asked.

"No, no, they're just standing—see? They're going back in now," I said, as part of the group headed back toward the door.

"We can stand out here and wait," he said. "The guy said there've been people leaving."

"Yeah I think the first band started early," I said. "This place is cool like that. They're done by 11pm. It's nice for me because I'm always tired with Victoria's schedule."

"Yeah, it didn't look like a nightclub in there."

"It's not," I said. "It's really laid back. And bands love playing there. I think the owner's a chef and he cooks for them."

"Quickest way to a man's heart," Mac said.

"Oh my gosh, Mac. Oh my gosh, oh my gosh. Go, go, go. Please catch that bus for us!"

Mac hopped to attention, looking over his shoulder at the bus I was staring at. The doors were closing and it was quite a ways off.

"You want to take the bus?" he asked, in a hurry as he was poised to run.

"B-bracelets," I said. "People with bracel—"

But I stopped speaking because Mac took off. The bus had already shifted and begun to move, but Mac was a professional athlete who made chasing a bus look easier than it actually was. He ran, maneuvering over concrete, patches of grass, and curbs like it was nothing. Mac made a bus chase look like something you'd see in the movies.

It was definitely not like that in real life, though. I knew because I was running behind him. I could see what he was doing, and I could feel what I was doing, and I knew they weren't the same things. I was a lot slower and it took all my strength and concentration to step in the right places and not fall or twist my ankle. I did my best to keep up with him so that I wouldn't leave him hanging once he caught the driver.

I smiled when I noticed the bus come to a stop. It took me several seconds to catch up to Mac, and by then he was already getting fussed at by the driver for making him stop.

Mac didn't waste any time. He pulled me onto the bus, and I stood there beside him while he dealt with the driver. I assumed he gave the guy more than the bus fare because he quit giving us a hard time.

There were about ten people on the bus, and only one of them was looking at us when we got on. She wasn't happy, so I didn't look at her long. I scanned the others, searching for the people I saw wearing bracelets.

And there they were—two women in the back of the bus. They had been at a distance, but I was almost sure they had on the bracelets we were looking for. I led Mac toward the back, holding on when I felt the bus shift and begin to move.

"Find a seat!" the driver yelled.

I moved quickly, going straight to the row of seats across from them, grinning when I realized I was correct about the bracelets.

"Would you be willing to sell us those bracelets?" I asked them after we sat down and I took a second to catch my breath. The girl next to the aisle looked at me, and I gestured to her arm. "If you're not planning on going back to that show," I said, clarifying.

"Oh me?" she asked, just understanding that I was talking to her. "You want this?" she said. "Are you going to the show?" She looked around a little like she was confused. (We were headed away from the venue, after all.)

"We actually ran and chased this bus to talk to you," I said. "The guy at the door told us we could go in if we could get our hands on a bracelet."

"Oh, definitely!" the girl next to her said, chiming in. "We don't need them anymore. We were just gonna throw them away." She instantly started tugging at her bracelet, making an exaggerated face like she was having a hard time getting it off.

"I have some scissors in my purse," I offered.

Within minutes, we made the exchange. We gave them a few dollars, and to our driver's annoyance, we got off at the next stop. We were a couple of miles from the venue by then, so we called a taxi to get back.

It was a lot of rigmarole for a ticket to see a band we didn't even know, but it was more for the adventure. I smiled at Mac once we got settled in the taxi. Mac sat next to the door, and I curled up next to him, so close that our bodies were touching.

I had some mom supplies in my bag, and I did a little surgery with our bracelets and band-aids. Mine fit perfectly, but Mac's needed a little extension, which I fashioned with the bandages. I expertly trimmed them and faced the altered part on the inside of our wrists. I have to say, I was pretty proud of my work. They looked completely unaltered from the outside and mostly unaltered from the inside. I finished Mac's bracelet and manually grabbed his wrist and turned it over so I could check the results. I had been concentrating on making the patch look good, so it was the first time that I noticed I was holding his hand.

I had control of his whole arm, and I stretched it across my body, thinking about how big and strong it was. I had never got this kind of physical reaction from touching a man. My fingertips were simultaneously numb and electric-feeling. I felt his muscles and bones, and I wanted to be this close to him for the rest of my life.

"Mac-key, M-m-m-mackey! You're my Mac, Mac, Mac-key!" I sang quietly so our cab driver wouldn't hear, but I did it dramatically, like I was singing him a whisper rock ballad.

"Wow, I have literally never had a song written about me before," he said, staring at me seriously when I finished.

He knew I was being silly, and his straight-faced reaction was also a joke.

"My daughter wrote that," I said. "I can't take the credit. I might owe her royalties from that part I sang just now."

"What do you mean she wrote it?" he asked.

I almost offered to show him the video, but at the last minute, I decided not to. I remembered the part where she said 'I love you' and I didn't want to give him any pressure. "My mom told me she was walking around the house saying Mackey like that, and singing a song about you after we left tonight."

He looked at me. "Your mom told you that?"

I nodded.

He closed his eyes and turned away, using his free hand to wipe at his face. It sort of looked like a worried gesture, the way he rubbed his eyebrows.

"Is it okay?" I asked.

"Yes," he said. "It's good."

"The Bing Room is up and on your right," the cab driver said. "I think this is as close as we're gonna get."

Mac paid the guy and we got out, walking down the sidewalk for half a block until we got to the door. Again, we opened it and we were greeted by the same guy who was staring at us, waiting to see our wristbands.

"You again, did you get one?" He asked the question as his eyes roamed to our wrists, and he just kept on talking. "Oh good, where'd you find it? Come on in, you guys." He stepped to the side, gladly letting us in.

"We had to ride a city bus down to Belmont and then a taxi back here," I said.

"Seriously?" the guy asked. He leaned in and spoke loudly over the music.

"Yes!" I said, smiling as we walked away. "Can you believe it? We had to chase a bus!"

I turned to focus on navigating the path in front of me. Mac was leading the way, and I reached out to take a hold of his arm. He felt me do it, and he reached out for me. I pulled him in, and we walked with our arms linked securely at our elbows.

The music was loud. The heavy bass rhythm shook my whole body. It was dark in there with colorful lights moving and blinking. I held onto Mac's arm as we walked, and I felt like there might as well be no other man in this room. I only had eyes for him.

He found a place for us to the right of the stage. We were standing with our backs to the wall, behind the crowd, but we could easily see the stage. Mac pulled me into his arms the minute he found a place to stand. I went to him, holding onto him in the chaotic darkness.

The music was soulful, and I felt myself making tiny movements, shifting with the beat. Mac went along with it, leading me in a tiny rhythmic motion. He knew how to find the beat. He knew how to dance. I could tell that already, and we were barely moving. We stayed like that, watching the band and holding onto each other, for the rest of the song which must have been five or six minutes.

A waitress came by as the band went into the second song, but we told her we were fine for the time being and might get something later. Mac had his back to the wall and I was positioned with my back to his chest. He leaned down so that he could speak near my ear.

"Do you like it in here?" he asked.

I nodded. "I do," I said, leaning into him. "How could I not?"

His face was near my cheek and neck, and I moved a little, letting my cheek brush against him.

"The music sounds good to me," I added. "Do you like it?"

Mac moved to speak near my ear again. "I like the music just fine, but there are other things about my current situation, Morgan, that I care about more than the music." He spoke slowly, and the words went into my ear and through my body, causing my insides to feel like velvet.

Goodness.

My senses were overwhelmed.

The music and the darkness, and the fact that Mac Klein was holding onto me was enough. *But whispering things like that into my ear?* It was just too much. My body was against his, and his arms were around me. It was packed in the Bing Room, and everyone was watching the band, so Mac and I were able to stand there and hold onto each other without anyone noticing or caring. It was intoxicating—the whole thing—the sound of the music along with the atmosphere and Mac's embrace.

We talked a little, but mostly we just stood there and watched the performance. Really, the show was second place to the feeling of being held by Mac. We got lost for what must have been an hour or more until the band announced that they were about to finish and that the closing band would be on soon.

I turned in Mac's arms, breaking away from him as my eyes met his. "I know you have camp Monday," I said. "I don't want to wear you out or drag you around too much. We could always go back to the house and hang out there. Victoria will be sleeping."

"You're not wearing me out, but I'm also good with heading back if you want to."

CHAPTER 16

My parents were still awake when we got to their house, and they came out to greet us. My mom said that Victoria was exhausted and fell asleep easily and then my dad admitted to giving her a root beer float when he got back from Rodney's.

The four of us stayed up and talked for a while. At first, we recounted things that happened at Rodney's house, and then Mac and I mentioned the band we saw at the Bing Room.

I told them we had to ask people for their wristbands to get in, but I didn't go into the whole thing about the bus and taxi rides. They would've enjoyed the story and I was fine with them knowing, but part of me just wanted to keep that part of our evening a secret.

I remembered watching Mac run like a superstar as he easily caught that bus. I figured maybe one day I'd share that story with somebody, but for tonight I was keeping it to myself. Mac took my cue and didn't mention it. We had enough to talk about, anyway.

My parents were up with us for a while before my mom finally said they should go to bed.

"Are you hungry?" I asked as soon as they disappeared down the hall.

"I'm not starving," Mac said.

"All right," I nodded. "I think we could start a movie, and if we get hungry, I'll get up and get us some snacks." I smiled. "Victoria would tell us to have popcorn."

The two of us kicked off our shoes, and went to the couch. I wanted to curl up next to Mac, so I told him I was going to change. I felt confident in my dress, but I opted for sweatpants and a T-shirt. I took a second to choose an outfit with colors that looked good together, but it was casual and comfortable and not fancy at all.

I had on loose but thin grey sweatpants with a fitted t-shirt that was yellow with a small vintage beach scene across the chest. It was warm outside, and I rolled the pants, making them into highwaters.

I walked with a spring in my step as I made my way barefoot back into the living room. Mac was sitting on the edge of the couch, staring down at his phone, and he turned it off and tossed it on the seat next to him when he saw me.

I bit my lip and felt embarrassed to cross the living room with him staring at me like that. He leaned back on the couch, casually watching me. I went over to him, only pausing to turn on the television before sitting down next to him on the couch.

I got to a random music station just for some noise. I set the remote on the couch and turned to look at Mac.

He smiled at me, reaching over. I thought he was reaching for the remote, but he took my hand instead. He pulled my arm into his lap, holding my hand with both of his, inspecting it.

"Oh, no, is that from today?" I asked, seeing his wrist as he moved.

On the backside of his arm was a bad bruise. It was deep, dark purple in one spot, and then there was a large lighter purple area around it. I pulled his hand into my lap so that I could inspect the injury.

Victoria had done this. She had tripped on a block today at the children's museum. She was balancing on a block, and with the way she fell, it could have been bad if Mac hadn't caught her. I had seen the heroic act by Mac, so I knew he had hit his arm when he grabbed her. But he didn't flinch or mention it when I asked him if he was okay.

"It's nothing," he said, pulling away a little like he wanted me to stop looking at it.

"I am so sorry," I said, being serious. It was a deep bruise, and it looked like it hurt.

"It's seriously nothing, Morgan. I'm glad I was standing there."

"Me too," I said. "I'm so thankful."

We sat there, with me curled up to him, holding hands and talking into the middle of the night. I wanted to walk him to the

Gilberts' house when we were finished, but he insisted that he would only want to walk me back after that, so I stayed at home.

We both knew he was leaving the following morning and because of it, I didn't get much sleep that night.

I woke up feeling unrested and unsettled. I had a pretty bad stomachache, and I didn't know if it was from the barbecue the night before or from all that worrying I had done during the early morning hours. I had to shake it off because I was the one taking Mac to the airport.

We had to leave the house by nine that morning, and we had plans to get together at eight so we had time to say goodbye. We stayed up really late, and my sleep had been restless, so waking up felt like a puffy-eyed dream.

I went through all the motions of acting happy but tired. I smiled at Mac and interacted with him and my family that morning. I acted normal and said and did normal things. I told Mac how much I would miss him and I held his hand.

Even when it was just Mac and me on the way to the airport, I was holding his hand and saying all the right things. But on the inside, I was stewing and brewing. I came to the conclusion, during my restless, nauseated sleep, that I needed to put things to an end with Mac before they went too far. It was just too much too fast.

I wanted to say it to his face, but I knew there was no way I could do it while he was in San Diego because he would want to stay and work things out. I needed to let him get back to his life before I said anything.

"Are you sure you're okay?" Mac asked when we were almost to the airport.

"Yeah, I'm just, you know... the arrival gate is always a lot more fun than the departure gate."

"Come to *my* arrival gate," he said.

I smiled—a fake one, but he didn't know. "I will," I lied.

We talked for a few more minutes, but I dropped him off in a bit of a hurry because there was a lot of traffic at the airport.

He kissed me, and I really wanted to enjoy it, but I was heartbroken and too preoccupied with pretending to enjoy the kiss to actually enjoy it.

I told Mac goodbye and then I cried on the way home. My mom was watching Victoria so I tried to get it together before I made it back to them, but it was difficult.

Victoria was preoccupied with toys but I ended up telling my mom about my decision to break things off with Mac. She couldn't understand, and she thought it was wise of me to reconsider, but I told her my mind was made up.

I went to my room and called his phone and left him a voicemail once I knew that he was in the air and had his phone switched off. Victoria could hear me, and she could tell that something was the matter and therefore gave me space.

I dialed his number and waited for the message.

I took a deep breath, anticipating the beep.

I spoke as soon as I heard it.

"Hey, Mac. I'm sorry. I'm sorry this is happening in a message. I didn't know what else to do. I knew that if I told you when you were still in California, you would stay here. But, hey, listen, I really do think it's better if we try to forget this weekend ever happened. I was thinking about that bruise and feeling so worried about you. You've got camp starting next week and you have to be in shape. Plus, I have Victoria 24-7. I realize all that running around probably wore you out when you were here, and that is every day with me. I have my parents to help me some, but I have her all the time. She's pretty much my constant compan—"

Beep!

I couldn't finish my message because it cut me off. I waited to hear the part about deleting the message because I would definitely have chosen to do that, but it never came.

"Goodbye," the robot voice said.

"Where's the delete option?" I asked out loud, regarding the phone in confusion.

As far as I could tell the message was sent, and I called right back.

"I'm sorry. I think that message sent. But Mac, I'm sorry. I worried and worried about your arm last night. I feel sick about it. I saw it happen, and I knew you hit your arm. It's not just that, though. I just have to look out for Victoria and me, and I think it's best. I know it is. I'm sorry, Mac. I reall—"

Beep!

"To listen to your message, press one."

The phone went through the steps this time, but I let the message go through. The first one was already sent, so I figured the second one needed to go as well.

I just hung up. I felt desperate. I didn't want him to get those messages and I also knew I had to do that. I put my phone away in my bedroom and went to spend the day with Victoria.

We went to pick out a replacement faucet for a tenant, and I didn't take my phone with me. Even after I got home from that errand, I still didn't go to my phone.

I didn't look at it for six hours that day, which felt like too long of a time. I expected to have a whole array of messages from Mac. I honestly thought, maybe I hoped, that Mac wouldn't be able to take 'no' for an answer. I imagined he would have called or texted several times.

But there was just one text message from him.

Mac: I made it home. Call me when you can.

I stared at it, blinking.

It almost seemed like he hadn't heard my messages—like there was nothing wrong. Or maybe he had heard them and this was still what he wanted to write. I didn't know what to do.

It broke my heart but I decided not to call him. He called me twice that evening, and I didn't pick up. I texted him another message that said how sorry I was, but that I just needed to take time for myself. I sent it, and I didn't hear back from him that night.

I felt like complete trash, honestly. Garbage. I was disgusted with myself for ending things. I was mad at myself, but I let myself get too close too fast and I got scared.

I hardly slept for the next few days. Mac called me every night and never left a message. Every night, I sent a text back to him that said two simple words, *I'm sorry.*

I went back to things the way they were before Mac came back into my life. But it wasn't good. It didn't feel right. I was depressed, and the only thing that got me through it was knowing that it was better for Mac. Playing in the NFL and raising a family is difficult, and I couldn't ask him to do it for someone else's child. I knew he was willing, but it was a lot, and I was just unwilling to hold him back.

Days passed. Mac still called a few times a week, but I didn't answer. I lost fifteen pounds in two weeks. I wasn't trying to be dramatic or starve myself, but I wasn't hungry. I had a stomachache, and for days, I couldn't think of anything that sounded good to eat. I ate little bites at a time.

I had been reading my Bible more. I tended to do that in times of distress.

I would love to say God spoke audibly to me every time I opened it, but that didn't happen. I felt encouraged and sustained by seeking God, but I never had a grand sense of relief or even full closure and peace about Mac.

One day, when I was feeling especially restless, I read a passage in the book of Matthew. I remembered it from before, but that day it hit me in a different way. It was the passage where a man was going on a journey and he gave talents to each of his servants to tend to while he was gone. The servant who got five talents multiplied it and gained five more. The servant who had two talents gained two more. But the one who was given one talent, buried it out of fear.

In the past, when I read that, I imagined it as literal talent, but today my heart saw the verse differently.

I knew that the talent was Mac and I was hiding him away, burying him out of fear. I was taking myself out of the game, just like the man with one talent. I read that verse, and I could see myself literally burying Mac, covering him at the beach with sand.

It was just enough to shake me out of my deception.

If I was ashamed of my choices, it was up to me to change them. I couldn't bury Mac. Any attempt at pushing him away was out of fear, and I just couldn't do that.

There was no reason for me to be the one to leave. If Mac thought it was best to not raise someone else's daughter, then let him be the one to leave. I was doing myself and my daughter a major disservice by burying this gift. I had done wrong, and I saw it clearly in the words of that story.

I told myself that if Mac called that night I would take his call happily. I told myself that I was going to beg him to let us start over.

CHAPTER 17

If Mac called, it was normally between six and seven in the evening. I had that epiphany about the talents at around two in the afternoon, while Victoria was taking a nap, and it was difficult to wait to see if he would call.

I wanted to call and tell him I had seen the error of my ways, but I didn't let myself do it. I was hoping for the best, but I still wanted to wait on him. He usually called me when he got done with camp for the day, and I didn't want to rush it while he was training.

I dragged Victoria around to run errands with me all morning and I had promised her that I would take her swimming next door that afternoon. I planned on doing it from four to five so that I could be out of the pool and watching for Mac's call in plenty of time.

Victoria was doing a great job with swimming. She was young, and I still stayed right next to her, but she knew how to swim. I went on YouTube about a year ago and learned how to give her lessons. We started coming over to the neighbors' pool twice a week to practice. I had been a confident swimmer since I was a little girl, and I wanted that for Victoria.

We stayed at the Gilberts' for an hour before towel drying and making our way through the yard and back to the house. I took a quick shower before I looked at my phone.

My heart dropped when I saw Mac's name on the screen. It wasn't even close to six, and he had already called. *How had I missed him already?* This was simply unacceptable. I would call him back immediately. My eyes saw that he left me a voicemail message before my brain could process the significance of that fact.

I pressed the buttons to listen to the message.

I put the phone to my ear while I absentmindedly combed Victoria's hair. I had helped her out of her wet swimsuit before I showered, but her hair was still wet and tangled and needed to be combed. She played quietly with her toy doctor kit, using stuffed animals as patients. I held the phone to my ear as I combed her hair.

"Hey, Morgan, this is Mac."

I pressed the phone to my ear and closed my eyes, my heart racing when I heard his voice. I could hear him take a deep breath.

"Okay, I need you to respond with something besides a text that says you're sorry. Please tell me what you're thinking.

I'm doing camp, and my days are full, but I'm just over here wondering where you are and what you're doing, Morgan. What happened? What did I miss? I thought we were happy we reconnected. Did I do something? I feel like we deserve to give this more of a chance. (He breathed a sigh.) Anyway, I wish you would call me and just expla—"

Beep!

He was clearly cut off, but there was not a second message. I listened to it again. He was serious and sincere, and his words pierced into my heart. *What were the chances that he would leave me a message on the day I was trying to talk to him?* I set down the comb, and Victoria went back to playing with her stethoscope and stuffed animals.

I was shaking visibly as I dialed the number to call him back. Tears filled my eyes as the phone rang. I didn't mean to be overwhelmed. I wished I could have kept it together, but it was impossible. Tears just started to flow. I held them back as best as I could as I waited for him to pick up.

"Hello?" he said. "Morgan?"

"Yes," I said, trying my best to sound normal even though I was actively crying.

"Morgan, what's going on?"

"I am so sorry, Mac." The words came out slowly and deliberately because I was trying to speak like I wasn't crying.

"Did you get my message?" he asked.

"Yes, but I was going to call before you ever left it," I said. "I was going to call you today, anyway." My voice came out more confidently this time because I knew I had to talk to him. I knew I had to explain. "Do you have a minute?" I asked.

Mac let out a humorless laugh. "Yeah, Morgan, I have a minute."

I sighed. "I was sick that last morning you were here. I don't know if it was stomach stuff or what—it kind of hasn't gotten all the way better yet, but it was bad that day. I think it's just worry. I know how much you put into football, Mac, and I knew we wore you out that day with the children's museum and everything. And it's just *every day* of that, you know? Then it was that bruise on your arm that really set me off. It looked like it really hurt, and it scared me."

"You told me that already," he said. "And I assured you I was fine. Imagine how Victoria would feel if she found out that she was the one who kept us apart. It would be like the thought of me keeping my mom and dad apart for tripping over a block one day. That would have been terrible for them, and unfair to me."

"I know, Mac I know it's wrong. I realize I was wrong. I've been thinking about nothing else all day. I am so sorry."

"So, what are you going to do about it?" he asked.

"I don't know. I didn't know you… whatever you want me to do."

"I want you here," he said without hesitation.

"When?"

"Now," he said, again without hesitating. "I'm going through camp, and every single day, I come home, and I wish you were at my house, Morgan."

My heart raced. I was so happy that I could start crying all over again. I blinked away the stinging tears.

"Yes," I said.

But he didn't hear me because he was already talking. "The apartment's livable now," he said. "They're finishing the tile in the bathroom and putting fixtures in. It's basically ready. And I have an extra bedroom in the house, anyway. I have plenty of room. And I have a pool for you and Victoria."

"Yes," I said again.

"Yes?"

"Yes. We'll go there. You do mean me *and* Tory, right? I'm only making sure because she would want to come."

He cleared his throat as I was talking. "Yes, Morgan. I know you come with your daughter. I want you both here."

"Then we will. We'll come. I'm sorry I hid this gift, Mac."

"You are? You will?"

"Yes."

"When? Soon?" he asked.

"Yes. As soon as I can."

"What are we talking? Weeks, days?"

"A section of the wall in the apartment complex had mold on it, so I'm dealing with a company about getting rid of it. That could take a couple of weeks, so..." I paused. "I'm just kidding,"

I added. "I do have someone coming to get rid of mold, but I'll deal with that from Seattle."

"Are you serious?"

"Yes."

"You're coming here?"

"Yes."

Mac let out an excited yell that made tears spring to my eyes. "You're saying that all I had to do was leave you a message? I should've done this a long time ago."

"I don't know if it would've worked on another day," I said. "Like I said, I was already planning on calling you today."

"What happened that made you want to do that?"

"I'm pretty sure I misinterpreted a Bible verse," I said, laughing a little.

"Well, misinterpreted or not, I'm not surprised that it was God who made you do it, because I was fed up. I was about to go to California to talk some sense into you—quit my job if I had to."

"I'm sorry. I thought we needed to break up for you," I said.

"Well, we don't," he said.

"Thank you," I said after a few seconds. "Do you think we could just pretend it never happened? Would it be possible to forgive me so much that we don't talk about it anymore?"

"I would love to not talk about it," Mac said.

"Great," I said. "Me too."

"Can you keep yourself from doing it again?"

"Yes. Can you trust me?"

"I hope so," he said. "Because, yes, I do trust you. I don't really care what happened to make you ignore me, as long as it's over."

"It is over, and I'm sorry. It was never about you. It was just me not wanting to bring you down."

I spoke quietly because Victoria was on the other side of the room. It didn't seem like she was listening to me, but I could never be sure with her.

"That's what you don't understand, Morgan. It's hilarious to me that you don't see it how I see it. You think you bring me down, and you're literally the only woman who does *not* bring me down. I'm funnier when I'm around you. You should ask my family. I've been in a terrible mood lately."

"Mac, Mac, I'm so, I'm happy you missed me, but I'm so sorry. I missed you so much every day. You are a gift to me, and I tried to reject it. Not reject you, and definitely not because I didn't want you, but—"

"I know," he said, cutting me off. "You don't have to say anymore. Especially if little ears are right there."

"They are," I said thankfully.

"What happened with the apartment and the mold issue?" he asked, changing the subject.

"It was back behind the hot water heater in one of the second-story units. I guess, at one point, there was a leak, and it just… it's tight in there, so it didn't dry out."

"Did you get someone to look at it?" he asked.

"Yeah, Darren, my handyman. He knows about plumbing and he said he's going to fix the whole area with some kind of special paint to kill that mold. He said if worse comes to worst we would have to get a dehumidifier, but I can't see how that would be the case since it's the same setup as in all the other apartments and no one else is having problems."

"Yeah, it's probably from that leak. I guess he'll check the floorboard or whatever's underneath that heater just to make sure nothing needs to be replaced."

"He will," I said. "He already mentioned that."

"Okay, so, is that all that needs your attention over there? Do you think you can do your other stuff from Seattle?"

"Yes. For how long?"

"Forever," he said. He let out a little laugh afterward. "I'm serious, but I know you can't do that."

"Victoria has art classes on Friday and a little pre-gymnastics class on Monday and Wednesday. And you know, I do the library thing on Tuesdays. Which, by the way, I read your mother's books to them these last two weeks. I took my autographed set up to the library and everyone was impressed. They all gathered around to inspect them. The teens in the homeschool group were especially excited about the Lox Island book."

"Oh yeah?"

"Yeah."

"Well, they have libraries in Seattle, too," he said.

I smiled because I absolutely loved it that he wanted me there. I wanted to go. "Oh, do they?" I asked.

"Yep. And art and whatever kind of gymnastics you were talking about. I'm pretty sure Seattle has all that. Plus, me and Victoria love each other. You can't keep us apart for a measly-old art lesson."

I wasn't going to agree to move two states away right that second, but I knew it would happen sooner than later. I felt desperate to get to Mac, and I could hear in his voice that he felt the same way.

"I'll try to book something for this Friday," I said. I wanted to leave that very night, but I figured I should give myself a day to pack and prepare.

Somewhere in my heart, I kind of figured I would never really be coming back to San Diego. I might make trips and be there temporarily, but I felt deep down that this was goodbye to any city that wasn't where Mac Klein lived.

Mac was a gift to me, and I meant to enjoy him to the fullest.

Chapter 18

I told Mac we would see him Friday afternoon when he got done with training camp. My flight actually landed at 10am, but I didn't give him the correct time because I wanted to surprise him somewhere out of the blue.

It was only a few hours earlier than he expected, but I wanted to plan a surprise. I knew he would react well to being taken off-guard, so I knew it would be fun. I had Katie's number saved in my phone, and I made a whole plan with her.

Victoria was not traveling with me just yet. My mother and father would fly up with her in a couple of days. My dad had his team doing conditioning, and he would take Monday off. He and Mom would fly here Sunday evening, spend the night, and turn around and go home Monday morning.

Essentially, they were just dropping off Victoria, but they could see and understand my resolve about being with Mac, and both of them wanted to see his place and know where we were going.

This worked out because it gave me a couple of days to see what was going on with our living situation before Victoria came. I didn't think of this as moving to Seattle, but I also no longer felt tied to San Diego. I knew it would be sad and hard leaving my parents, but my heart was with Mac.

I went from being devastated and faking happiness to being so elated that I had to fake it the other way now. I didn't want my parents to think I didn't care about them, but I was jumping out of my skin to get to Mac.

I planned to go in half a day early so that I could surprise him at the field instead of him picking me up at the airport after work. If my father wasn't Les Lake, this would have never happened, but as it stood, the Seattle Seahawks gave me VIP treatment in their training room so that I could pull off my surprise for Mac.

My dad had contacted them the day before, and the coach said that they had all heard about me from Mac. Based on whatever Mac said about me, they knew he would be happy with a surprise. And they all loved Mac so much that they got really into it.

Everyone came up with an elaborate plan to surprise him. The coaching staff had it worked out by the time I got there. I was hoping to do something really simple and low maintenance like jump out from behind a corner, but they had other plans.

They would get Mac to be one of the players chosen this week for the press conference. There would be three players and the head coach, and they would take about thirty minutes of questions.

I was supposed to pose as a reporter in a crowd of about ten or twelve others. I worked with a woman named Patty. She was once in charge of the team's laundry and uniforms, but now she did so much more. Every club needed a Patty. She knew everything. She was close to Mac, and she got really into the whole surprise.

She had someone waiting for me, ready to help me with my hair and makeup. They even gave me a tape recorder and some glasses to help me look the part. I had brought a blue pantsuit that Patty said would suffice. If things worked out with my disguise Mac wouldn't know I was there until I asked him a direct question.

I was thankful, and granted it was really sweet of her to take so much time to think of an elaborate plan, but the press conference was one hundred percent real, and that was a nerve-racking thought for me.

I went with it, though, because what else was I going to do? There was just no way I could go against the plan. Everyone was already in on it.

Katie was even there. She had been the one to pick me up at the airport, and she stayed to see the surprise. She stayed behind the scenes with Patty so that Mac wouldn't be tipped off.

Patty's friend, a rather tall, flamboyant lady named Lorraine, teased, combed, and sprayed my hair just right so Mac would never recognize me. She even used some sort of high-tech temporary spray that made it look lighter than it was.

I looked blonder than normal, and it actually looked pretty natural. I honestly looked like a different person when Lorraine was finished with me. I wouldn't have even recognized myself.

We knew where Mac was going to be sitting, so I positioned myself where a man was in front of me. I could look at Mac on my own terms without being exposed to him. The plan was for me to let the whole interview take place and then get his attention at the end of it.

I was thankful for that because it gave me time to settle down. I would wait for the right time and then say, "Mister Klein, what do you plan on doing when we leave here today?"

Patty's idea was for me to say a bunch of stuff (about football, and in character) before getting his attention with something personal. But I dwindled it down to one single question and Patty went with it. She knew I didn't want to make a big deal about it, and we were already doing a lot more than I expected.

Mac came in with the head coach and the other players. I was so glad I had plans to wait until the end of the press conference to surprise him. He came into the room, and I was so nervous that it took ten minutes to regulate my breathing and talk myself into believing that everything was okay. I grew up in this environment, and I had been to these before, but this one was different.

I listened to the players and coach, taking fake notes and carefully avoiding Mac's gaze as I tried to imitate the rest of the journalists. I even squinted my eyes and made a little face in case he caught a glimpse of me.

"Is there anything else?" The coach asked after a while.

That was definitely my cue.

I knew if he asked that, they were about to shut it down.

I didn't even give myself time to think about it. If I thought about it I would doubt it, and if I doubted it, I would back out. I shifted to the side a foot or two, making sure Mac could see me when he glanced up. I cleared my throat.

"Excuse me, this question is for number eight Mac Klein, what do you plan on doing later toni—"

But I could not finish because Mac noticed me and he suddenly snapped to attention. He slapped his hands down on the table, causing multiple people to gasp. I watched his face change and I kept my eyes trained on him as he got to the edge of his seat in a sudden quick jerky movement that made someone else gasp again.

Mac was intense. He was funny that way. He was an easygoing guy who had already made everyone laugh a couple of times in this press conference. But he was also intense, and that came out when he saw me. He jumped again, staring at me with the most intense expression he had ever given me.

I couldn't think straight, so I just smiled and gave him a little wave from across the table.

"What? Are you kidding me?" Mac shook his head, holding back astonished, happy tears at the sight of me, which made me feel like I needed to cry. He was shocked. He had no idea I was in that room this whole time, and he was obviously excited. Everyone could see the truth in his reaction. Mac let out a yell as he stood up, and he did a little jig before jumping over the table. This caused another round of gasps, including one from me.

None of us expected him to spring over the table. It was amazing because it wasn't like he freaked out and made a big deal about it. He just effortlessly sprang over it, using his hand for leverage as he popped over to the other side.

He landed on his feet in front of several reporters. There were just a few feet between us now, and he covered that space quickly, dancing again as he moved. Oh, this boy had charisma. He didn't stop until he had reached me and had me in his arms. He scooped me up, holding me tightly, squeezing my body to his.

"What the Samuel Hill are you doing here, my girl? How did you get here?" he asked the question quietly where no one could hear.

"Surprise, I'm early," I said, in his ear as we hugged. I was smiling because I was happy to see him, but I was also nervous because all eyes were on us. I had no idea how I would gracefully get out of there and let them wrap up our interview. No one told me what to do once I got his attention.

Thankfully, I didn't even have to worry about it. Mac set me down, and then, before I could think or do anything, he stooped down. He let out another excited yell as he aimed his shoulder for my midsection and suddenly I was swept off of my feet.

"I think we were done here, anyway," Mac said, standing up with me over his shoulder. He bowed. I could feel it. I also felt him wave. "Thank you all. Thank you, Coach. See you bright and early in the morning for those sprints."

"Have fun!" someone said.

I assumed it was his coach because it sounded like him, but it was difficult to discern with my head upside down and my hair in my face.

Mac walked out instantly. He set me to my feet as soon as we walked out of the conference room. Patty and Katie, along with several other people were standing on the other side of the door like they had been listening.

"Mac Klein, did you just carry this girl out of there over your shoulder?" Patty asked in a motherly tone.

"Yes ma'am, I did," Mac admitted, straightening himself.

"Are they even done with the interview?"

"No ma'am. But almost." Mac took my hand, securing it in front of his chest. He moved like he was poised to take off with me in his grasp. "Oh, hey Katie," he said.

"Hey," she said, wide-eyed and smiling at her brother.

"Hey, we're leaving. You drove Morgan up here, I assume?" He shifted to look at me. "Where's Victoria?"

"She stayed back with Mom and Dad. They're flying her here on Sunday."

"Are they all coming?" he asked.

I nodded, and he nodded back at me.

"We'll talk about it on the way home." He looked at his sister. "Where'd you park? Are you close?"

"Yeah, and I'm coming with you."

"Okay, come on," Mac said in a friendly but no-nonsense tone. He waved at everyone else. "Bye, you guys, Miss Patty. Thank you to whoever had a hand in this." He adjusted me in his arms. "You know this is my girl, right?"

"I figured you liked her a little bit after you walked out with her over your shoulder like a sack of flour." Patty smiled at him. "She's a lovely young woman," she added.

"And Les Lake's daughter," someone else said.

"Yes ma'am, she is, thank you."

Patty gestured to the door. "How did it go in there?"

"He came out with her over his shoulder, so I'd say it went pretty good," that second person said.

"Was he surprised?" Patty asked, looking at me.

"He was so surprised," I said, smiling.

I held onto Mac's arm. I was out of it with all the commotion and could hardly appreciate how relieved I was to be standing next to him.

Patty's eyes widened suddenly and her head sunk below her shoulders like she was listening for something. "Go on and get out of here," she said, hurriedly. Her hands came up and she stepped toward us, almost shooing us away. "I hear them coming."

We took off in a hurry, and seconds later we heard the door open up. I glanced back as we jogged down the hall and noticed the players and coach coming out of the conference room. Patty would run a little interference.

"Where are we going?" I asked as we walked down another long hallway.

"Home. Bank Street," Mac said.

"Are you done for the day?" I asked.

"He is now," Katie said, smiling. She was adorable—light hair and light eyes. She and Mac were half-siblings, but they never talked about that. I only took note of it at this moment because their coloring was different. I could see common shapes in their facial features, though.

"I was done, anyway," Mac said as we walked. "That interview was all I had to do before I was on my way out."

There were long hallways with concrete walls that gave way to more long hallways with glass walls that finally took us to the entrance. I didn't care about my surroundings, honestly. My hand was securely in Mac's, and everything else seemed inconsequential.

Chapter 19

My life had a lot of excitement recently. I had run off to Seattle to be with a man I knew as a child. I was in love, and because of it, I was suddenly juggling all sorts of new situations and decisions.

Victoria wasn't with me on this trip, which was rare and odd. My mom reflexes were still turned on and I had to remind myself that I could relax and enjoy this weekend for what it was.

So, I had a lot going on already.

That was why I was not at all prepared for what happened next.

I spent one night in Mac's apartment, which I loved. It was a two-bedroom place, that was actually roomier than I anticipated based on how he talked about it.

The apartment was great, but that wasn't the amazing part of my morning.

Someone had uploaded a video of me surprising Mac at the press conference, and it was apparently going viral. I woke up to about twenty messages from friends and family saying that a video of me was all over the internet. My mom even texted to let me know she had seen it on Facebook.

Mac and I had stayed up really late last night, so it was 9am when I woke up and saw all of this. It happened literally overnight. I thought even overnight sensations took a while to catch before they went viral. I thought certain internet people had to blog about it and share it first.

I blinked at the screen, scanning the messages and feeling confused.

I found a text from my friend, Tristan, that had a link to the video. It was an official video from the team. I watched it, and oh, my heart.

Mac. He was the most precious, adorable, sweet but macho man that had ever lived. Tears stung my eyes as I watched the video of what happened.

His face.

His reaction.

His excitement was glorious.

He made his emotions known… surprise, happiness, relief, excitement, and love. His happiness was contagious, and I was rooting for the man in the video even though I had been there and seen it live the first time.

He was so handsome that if I wasn't the girl in the video, I'd feel jealous of her. My phone rang while it was in my hand.

It was my mother, and I answered it the instant I saw her name because Victoria was with her.

"Hello?"

"My goodness, Morgan, did you get my messages? Did you see your video all over Facebook? Gene and Kristen even saw it all the way over in London. She said it's showing up on the trends or whatever you call it." Mom paused, but then quickly asked, "Are you there?"

"Yes, Mom, I just… is Victoria okay?"

"Oh, yeah, she's fine. She's in there playing with the little neighbor girl."

"I'm fine, too, I'm just… I just woke up. I was up late last night and I just opened my eyes. I was thinking about going back to sleep but then I saw all these messages."

"Did you even know your video made the news? I mean you looked like you were in a newsroom when it happened. Surely, you knew you were being videoed. Did you surprise him? That's what it looked like. I didn't know you were going to do that. Victoria talked to you last night, and you didn't mention it."

"It was a thing Mac's friends planned for me. His team wanted to surprise him so they set all that up."

"Oh, well it worked! Mac was just the cutest thing in that video. Baby, he loves you so much."

"I know, Mom. That's why I'm here."

"What are you going to do if that video keeps getting famous? Kristen was telling me you'll probably end up going on a talk show or something."

"Mom, I literally have no idea. I need like three minutes to wake up and process all this. I picked up the phone to make sure Victoria was doing okay."

"She's fine. She saw that video of her mom and she said, *what happened to her hair?*"

I laughed. "A lady named Lorraine did that. It was some kind of spray."

"Victoria was talking about how tall it was, but it did look lighter, now that you mention it."

I refreshed the YouTube page as I was sitting there talking to my mom, and the video had thousands more views than it did a minute ago.

Mac had to go to a morning workout, so I knew he wouldn't be back until noon. I wondered if he knew any of this was happening.

Another text came in as I was contemplating the unexpected turn my morning had taken.

I spent the afternoon and evening with Mac and his many roommates yesterday. We had a good time, talking about the fact that I surprised him at work. I told them everything Patty wanted me to say and we got a good laugh about that.

We knew my surprise had been a success.

We talked about it at dinner that night with Justin, Katie, Ozzy, and Bri who were all curious about me and wanted to hang out. We told them how great it was and that someone would surely post it some time since multiple cameras were rolling.

But none of us expected this.

After I spoke with my mom, I went through my messages, responding briefly to them. Everyone was saying how they saw the video. Some sent links to the video or screenshots of it. A couple of them were friends I hadn't talked to in a while, and they were wondering who Mac was and when we met.

It took me about ten minutes to quickly respond to them, and then I put down my phone and went to get dressed.

I started to make myself a cup of coffee, but I decided to walk over to the main house first, just in case anyone was up and had already made some over there. They were a hospitable bunch and I knew a visit from me would be well-received.

I put on some jeans and tied my hair up in a bun on top of my head. I went ahead and put on a little makeup since I didn't know if I would have another chance once Mac got done with his workout.

"Mac's page is blowing up because of that video," was the first thing out of Ozzy's mouth when I walked into the house that morning. "He's gained twenty thousand followers this morning. It's unbelievable. I've never seen anything like it. Look at my phone!"

Ozzy was sitting cross-legged on the couch and he gestured to the coffee table where his phone lit up with notification after notification.

"I'm just going to have to turn it off and check it again later," he said.

I made some coffee and spent the morning with Mac's family. I got along great with all of them. They were artsy and smart and they were fun to be around. Katie and their cousin, Bri, were both kind to me, going out of their way to include me and welcome me into their girls' group.

We did our best to turn off the media storm that was now brewing around us, but now and then, we would check the internet and find some new development.

The video was being shared and viewed at an unbelievable rate. Mac had natural swagger and rhythm, and he made movements doing a little celebration dance when he saw me. People set that part to music, and the video became a meme.

Mac was so lovable it wasn't even funny. The NFL already knew it, but now the rest of the world knew it, too. There was talk about who I was. Some people thought that I was a journalist who had captured Mac's heart, and others said I was his girlfriend posing as a journalist.

There were comments galore, and I quickly learned that maybe it was best if I didn't look at them. Mac was a charismatic human and women were in love with him at first sight. I laughed about it with everyone, and it was fine, but I also stopped reading the comments.

I hung out with Katie and Bri, and Ozzy kept us posted about the numbers, which were astounding. The video had almost a million views by noon. It was around that time when Ozzy came up next to Bri and me to show us something on his phone.

He settled between us in the kitchen and tilted the screen so that we could get a good look at it.

I could see from one glance that it was Lexi Brooks. She was a fun-loving ex-actress whose afternoon talk show was one of the most popular television shows in America.

Lexi had a weekend segment that she posted on her social media where she reacted to a couple of the latest internet videos or trends. These segments were funny and nearly as popular as her talk show. I had seen dozens of them come across my feed.

My heart started pounding, and I glanced at Ozzy who shook the phone like he was telling me to look at it.

He hit play in the middle of Lexi talking about a different video, one of a cat that was best friends with a rhino. I stared at the video, watching the two animals and wondering what was going on.

"It's right after this," Ozzy said. "Her producers are on top of things. She's the first person to do a segment with it."

"Does she show our video or something?" I asked.

"Yes, just watch it," Ozzy said. "She'll post this on her social media tonight, and we'll get about five million views from it."

It panned to Lexi, who was sitting at her home desk where she always sat for this segment.

"Okay, this next one is soooo good! Let's check out this dude that's about to win the hearts of all the romantics in the world. Okay, get this, the Seattle Seahawks released a video of one of their players, quarterback Mac Klein, who jumped over a table during a press conference to make out with one of the reporters." She made a face and raised her eyebrows. "I love this video. This one is my absolute favorite from this week. I think this is one of the most adorable things I've ever seen. This guy, Mac, he is just too… he actually puts the woman over his shoulder and… well, let's just watch it."

The screen panned to the video and you heard my muffled question to Mac and then saw Mac's whole reaction. I had seen the whole thing on video playback about ten times by now, and it never got old.

I grinned while it played. Mac was wonderful. He was so excited to see me that it was touching. He whooped and danced and sprang over that table like the floor was a trampoline.

The video finished, and the screen shifted back to Lexi's face. She was pretending to cry and wipe her eyes, and then she pretended to get caught. She was really good at her job and it was funny. Bri and I both laughed.

"That is seriously the best thing I have seen all week," Lexi said. "A-plus-plus for Mac Klein of the Seattle Seahawks. You really know how to sweep a woman off her feet, sir. We're swooning from this video." Lexi waved the index card she was holding, using it as a fan to cool herself off. Then she leaned back in her chair and carelessly tossed the index card. "This video is about to blow up," she said confidently, coming back to her desk to focus. "I could watch it twenty more times. I would love to have this pair on my show next week if we can make that happen."

CHAPTER 20

Two days later, I found myself sitting next to Mac in the backseat of a blacked-out Mercedes sedan on my way to the Lexi Brooks show. The driver had been waiting for us at the airport.

We didn't make plans until Sunday, and it was Monday (the following day) when they wanted us to appear on the show. It would be recorded live with a studio audience in the morning and then aired that afternoon. They were a current, up-to-date show and they wanted us there right away. They wanted to be the first to report the story.

Mac and I contemplated whether or not we wanted to go. Mac thought he should stay focused and stay at training camp, but the Seattle organization begged him to reconsider. They were watching the numbers on this video and they knew from a business standpoint they needed to capitalize on the video's momentum.

Our trip was rushed. We would only spend one night in Los Angeles, but we had first-class accommodations. My parents pushed back their trip to Seattle. They would come in on Wednesday and leave on Thursday. My dad would have to take two days off work instead of just one, but we were all making some adjustments in light of the video's success.

All of this was so unexpected and overnight that it could easily be overwhelming. But I never felt overwhelmed, not with Mac by my side. We were scheduled to film the Lexi show that morning, and then we had to go to a radio station that afternoon to be on the Five O'clock Live While You Drive show, which was recorded in L.A. but had millions of listeners worldwide. I was used to being around the spotlight with my family in the NFL, but this was the first time that it felt like the spotlight was shining directly on me. I had to respond to questions and make statements regarding things besides football, which was new to me.

The last time I checked, our video had six million views.

"Are you okay with everything?" Mac asked as we pulled onto the studio lot.

Our timing was so tight that we had to go straight there from the airport.

"I'm fine," I said, hoping to talk myself into believing it. "Are you good?"

"I'm great," he said. "It's an adventure, right? I mean, it's not like we can say the wrong thing. We're not bringing up hard topics. I'm sure they'll show us a list of questions."

Mac was right about that. They did give us the questions. Not only did they have Lexi's questions written down, but they had example answers for us that were witty and well thought-out.

Mac and I had no clue what to expect, and we got a good kick out of the suggested script. Mac told me all that was just a suggestion and that we would ultimately answer however we wanted.

I followed his lead. I was so out of my element that I probably would have sat there and memorized that script word-for-word had he not been there to reassure me it was more casual than that.

Mac held my hand through it all. Literally. He wasn't obnoxious with PDA, but he tried to maintain some sort of contact with me if he could. I was thankful for that because this was a lot to take in. He was confident and sure, and he smiled and spoke to everyone at the Lexi show like he knew them already. He was a friend to everyone, and I tried to match his self-assuredness with a quiet confidence of my own.

Mac was lovable, and I did my best to mimic that. He brought out the best in me. I didn't change my personality or anything, but I saw how he touched the lives of people around him, and I found myself speaking to people I normally wouldn't.

All this to say we were friendly with the backstage crew at the Lexi show. They helped us a lot in what would have otherwise been a complete whirlwind.

I felt like I was in a dream when they ushered us out to Lexi Brooks. They announced our names, and the audience erupted in applause.

Mac walked, he held my hand, leading the way, and waving to the audience. They loved him. Most of the audience was women, and they absolutely loved him. I didn't feel threatened, but I couldn't help but notice all the female screams as we walked to our place, standing in front of the couch.

Lexi shook both of our hands and then gestured for us to have a seat. "Well, aren't you two just the sweetest couple ever," she said, looking us over like she was some sort of inspector. The audience laughed, and she continued announcing. "Mac and Morgan became internet celebrities this weekend with a video the Seattle Seahawks released of Mac being surprised during a press conference. It's one of my favorites, you guys! For those who haven't seen it, let's go ahead and roll it one time."

The tech team was first class, and the second Lexi called for the video, the lights went down and it played on the gigantic screens in the studio. It was loud, and I could feel my heart pounding in my chest as I watched the whole video, this time with a studio audience full of people.

They all reacted as if it was their first time seeing it, and they laughed and made noises of approval during various places in the video.

Watching a whole group of people react to it was a crazy experience. Watching them felt like being on a roller coaster. They cheered when it was over, and I smiled at Mac.

"What was going on here, Mac?" Lexi asked as their applause trailed off. "I gather that you were at a press conference with your team, and your girlfriend surprised you there, right?"

"Exactly," Mac said. "She was sitting in the back. We'd already been in there for thirty minutes with no one coming in or out, so Morgan was the last person I expected to see." Mac smiled and shook his head. "It took me by surprise."

"Yeah, we see that," Lexi said. "Your reaction was absolutely wonderful! I think we all wish somebody would get that excited to see us."

"Mac has never had a problem with showing his feelings," I said, causing people to laugh.

"How long have you two been a couple?" Lexi asked.

"We met when we were kids," Mac said.

"That's what I hear," Lexi said, nodding. "Your father was coaching college football?"

"That's right," I agreed. "We were childhood friends when my dad coached in Nebraska, and then we got in touch again recently."

"And was this video the first meeting since you were children?" Lexi asked.

"No, we had seen each other before that," Mac said. "If I hadn't seen her since we were kids, I'm not sure if I would have recognized her—especially with the hair and makeup like it was. But, no, when this was filmed, I hadn't seen her in a few weeks, and I wasn't expecting her in that room, that's for sure."

Lexi looked down, shifting through a few cards. "I have all sorts of notes on you two. Morgan's dad is an NFL coach down in San Diego with the Chargers. And, whoa, here's a good one, Mac's mom, so it seems, was on our show a few months ago. She was doing promo for Lox Island, which she *wroooote!*" Lexi spoke dramatically and screwed her face up like she just couldn't believe what she was saying, and the audience cracked up. "Seriously, Mac's mother is *Lucy Klein*. Who, by the way, is so cool."

"Well, thank you," Mac said. "I remember her telling me about coming on your show."

"Oh yeah, what'd she say about it?" Lexi asked. She waved her hand and shook her head like she changed her mind. "Don't tell me if she said something bad."

All of this was officially off-script. We were now just sitting there having a conversation.

Mac sat up in his seat a little as he shook his head. "It was all really good," he said. "She had a great time over here." Mac made a serious expression and stared at Lexi. "She did say you guys treated her to a big steak dinner that night." He was only kidding and Lexi knew it, but he acted totally serious which was funny.

"Oh, we've got something way better than that," Lexi said. "After the season's over, which I guess is next spring, right?"

"Yes," Mac said.

She gave him a nod. "Well, next spring, we're going to send the two of you on a romantic getaway to a gorgeous beach house in Hawaii. (The audience cheered.) I've been to this place myself, and let me just tell you… you're gonna love it. I don't want people to know it exists, that's how nice it is. You'll have all the steak you can eat over there."

"I was only kidding about the steak," Mac said.

"I know you were," Lexi said. "Because we didn't buy your mom a steak dinner." She looked at the producer with a comically confused expression. "I don't think we did. Did we?"

Everyone laughed. It was a mostly rhetorical question, but a producer yelled out. "I think we did!"

"We actually did, it seems, buy your mom a steak dinner," Lexi said, correcting herself. She was making a face and being funny, and everyone laughed. Her face broke into a knowing grin. "No, seriously, we would love to get you two lovers a steak dinner tonight. And I'm serious about that vacation to the beach. I'm sending you on a romantic getaway."

She raised her eyebrows and everyone cheered. Mac looked at me and smiled and then shifted to look at Lexi with a little shrug.

"Sounds like a honeymoon."

"Oh, are you two getting married?"

Mac grinned and lifted one shoulder. "Well, I guess we are now."

The audience laughed again. Mac had them in the palm of his hand. I said a few things during that interview, and I smiled the whole time, but I was happy to let Mac take the lead. He was a man in every sense of the word, and I was proud to sit next to him.

Lexi was known for giving things away on her show, so we both knew she was serious about the trip. Neither of us expected her to do that which made for some funny exchanges during the remainder of our interview.

***

"As I see it, we're on a timer, right?" Mac said later that night as we sat on the couch together, eating dessert.

We were on the heels of a crazy, busy day, and it was finally time to relax. It was 8pm, I was in Mac's room, and we had just gotten room service for dinner.

"A timer for what?" I asked, after chewing a bite of chocolate mousse.

"Well, I mean, the Lexi show. The trip will be in April, probably, so we'll want to think about maybe, you know…"

He trailed off, but I didn't know where he was going with that, so I said, "Maybe what?"

"I mean, we should probably just assume we'll get married by then. Right?"

I could tell he was serious, and my heart started beating faster.

"I don't just want you guys in the guesthouse," he said. "It's fine for now but I want you with me, in my house, in my room."

We stared into each other's eyes, and I knew he was serious. I knew he wasn't changing his mind. Mac kissed me. His warm mouth covered mine, and my body felt weak from it.

"Okay," I said. "By April it is, then. I guess we're on a timer."

"Yeah, that's what I'm saying. I'll be okay with you in my guesthouse, but there's no way I am staying with you in a romantic house on the beach in Hawaii—not if we're not married. One man can only handle so much temptation. In fact, from where I stand right now on the temptation charts, I think we could go ahead and bump it up to this weekend."

I laughed at him and then I leaned in for a kiss. It was sticky and warm, and it made me think that getting married this weekend wasn't such a bad idea.

Epilogue

Mac

The following April

So, the timer had been set for April when the happy couple would take a trip together.

They made it in plenty of time. Mac and Morgan got married in November. Morgan and Victoria stayed in his guest house until the wedding, at which point, they moved into the main house. They needed to do it by April, and Mac would have done it instantly, so he figured November was splitting the difference.

They flew to Galveston for the wedding. Morgan got to see the original Bank Street and meet all of Mac's family. She thought of the Seattle house as the *Bank Street* house, so Bank Street in Galveston seemed like the second one to her even though it was the original.

Morgan loved seeing Mac's hometown, though. They got married during the season, so they scheduled it for a bye week.

His family was much larger than hers, so it was easier for her family to travel.

Mac's mom got her original illustrator to draw the pair as Garden City characters as a wedding gift. They were badgers in the artwork. They looked like themselves, except in badger form. It was one of their favorite gifts.

They also got a gorgeous painting from Mac's Aunt Tess who was a famous Texas painter. That painting was one of Mac's favorites as a child, and he teared up when she gave it to him.

Mac was thinking about that piece of art because he had just hired someone to paint a whole room to match it. He just saw it on Facetime. This was a surprise for his wife, which she would see when they got back to Washington.

The couple was on their Lexi-Brooks-sponsored trip to Hawaii, and it was every bit as wonderful as Lexi made it out to be.

Mac had a successful year. His team just fell short of going to the Super Bowl, which was a little heartbreaking because it would have been their third consecutive trip there. Mac took it well, though. He had played enough games to know that you couldn't do anything about a loss after it was in the books. All you could do was learn from it.

Of course, Mac wanted to win the Super Bowl every year he played. That had happened only once in his career, and even then, he was more fortunate than most. Mac didn't let it get him down when his season ended. He went on, training for the next season. He was healthy and playing well, and if he stayed on this path, he figured he had at least three more years in the league. He planned on staying in Seattle if they would have him, and that was fine with Morgan.

She and Victoria fit into his life like they had always been there. Morgan moved into his bedroom, and Victoria took over the nearest bedroom. They switched places with Justin, who moved into the guest house.

Justin had an amazing season this year, which came along with all sorts of sponsorships. He could definitely afford a place of his own, but he had gotten close to Mac and the rest of the crew, so he decided to stay on Bank Street for a while longer.

Justin was in on the babysitting this weekend. The whole gang was keeping Victoria while Mac and Morgan were on their trip. Both of their mothers were willing to fly in and watch her, but Katie had gotten close to the little girl, and so had everyone else who was living at the house. Katie was the main one in charge, but she had help from all three of the others.

It had been three days, and so far, everyone was doing fine. Mac and Morgan had two more days in Hawaii before they would head back.

Hawaii was unbelievable. Mac had beaches in Galveston, and Morgan had beaches in San Diego, but this was different. This was a tropical paradise, and Lexi set them up in the nicest house ever.

It was an unbelievable place with a view and a chef who cooked all their meals for them. The Lexi show had requested an update, and Mac knew they planned on doing that, but otherwise, they were off the grid. Off the grid to everyone but Victoria. They talked to her once a day to check in, so it didn't surprise Morgan when she walked into the living room to find Mac on Facetime, talking to the little girl.

"Here's your mama," Mac said, talking to Victoria. "Love you. Hug Aunt Katie and everyone else for us."

"Okayyyy!" she said. "I love you, big Dad."

"I love you, little daughter!" Mac said, calling out to the screen as Morgan took it away.

"Hey, cupcake, what are you doing?"

"Nothing. And that man didn't paint your room blue where your table is today."

"What?" Morgan asked.

Katie took the phone away from Victoria.

"Nothing," Katie said in a hurry.

She whispered something to Victoria. Morgan couldn't see or hear them.

"But nooo, I didn't tell her the secret," Victoria said at full volume. "I told her they *didn't* paint that room."

"What room didn't they paint?"

"You might as well show her!" Mac yelled, laughing.

"Show me what?" I asked staring at the screen.

"Let's go show her!" Katie said. "Mac said it was okay."

Mac watched his wife watch the screen. He smiled at her as she stared expectantly at it.

"Okay, okay, okay," Victoria said dramatically. "I wasn't gonna tell you it was painted blue like you wanted it to go with your new picture."

Morgan's face lit up as the girls aimed the camera at the new dining room. Morgan kept saying she wanted to paint the dining room blue to match that painting Tess had given them at their wedding.

Mac had hired someone to give the whole dining room a makeover. The paint job was only part of it. The new table was to be delivered tomorrow. Thankfully, Victoria didn't know about it so she couldn't spill the beans.

Mac watched as Victoria gave Morgan the grand tour of the paint job. It took them about three minutes, and Morgan got off the phone, thanking Katie and telling them all she loved them.

She looked at Mac when she hung up the call.

She stared at him. Her eyes were golden, like honey, and he thought she tasted like honey, too.

"A blue room? What the actual Samuel Hill did you do to my house?" she asked in a flirty tone.

Samuel Hill had made it into their repertoire of inside jokes, and Mac grinned at her for saying it.

"Do you like it?" Mac asked.

Morgan's eyes were sparkling with delight as she looked at him. "It's the best dining room anyone has ever had. Did you see how that blue goes with the floors? I don't know how you got it so perfect, baby, I'm in love."

She turned and twisted and wiggled her way into his lap, and Mac smiled as he made room for her.

"Was it supposed to be a surprise?" she asked.

"Yes. And she was hilarious trying not to tell you. Did you hear her? She thought she'd specifically inform you that *no one* had painted the dining room."

Morgan laughed. She reached up and touched the side of his face. She was sitting on his lap, and she licked her lips before kissing him. They both had on swimsuits, and her skin was gloriously sticking to his. Mac could not get enough of this woman. He was just as fascinated by her today as he was when he was ten years old. He knew it would be that way for as long as he lived.

The End

(till book 8)

Thanks to my team ~ Chris, Coda, Jan, Glenda, Yvette, and Pete